There I Find Light
Strawberry Sands Book Seven

Jessie Gussman

Published By: Jessie Gussman

This is a work of fiction. Similarities to real people, places, or events are entirely coincidental. Copyright © 2023 by Jessie Gussman.

Written by Jessie Gussman.

All rights reserved.

No portion of this book may be reproduced in any form without written permission from the publisher or author, except as permitted by U.S. copyright law.

Contents

Acknowledgements	V
Note from Jessie	1
1. Chapter 1	3
2. Chapter 2	9
3. Chapter 3	14
4. Chapter 4	17
5. Chapter 5	23
6. Chapter 6	33
7. Chapter 7	40
8. Chapter 8	50
9. Chapter 9	58
10. Chapter 10	63
11. Chapter 11	70
12. Chapter 12	78
13. Chapter 13	82
14. Chapter 14	87
15. Chapter 15	93
16. Chapter 16	100
17. Chapter 17	109
18. Chapter 18	115

Epilogue	124
There I Find Patience	126
A Gift from Jessie	133

Acknowledgements

Cover art by Kim Killion of The Killion Group
Editing by Heather Hayden
Narration by Jay Dyess
Author Services by CE Author Assistant

Listen to the unabridged audio for FREE performed by Jay Dyess on the Say with Jay channel on YouTube. Get early access to all of Jay's recordings and listen to Jessie's books before they're available to the general public, plus get daily Bible readings by Jay and bonus scenes by becoming a Say with Jay channel member.

Note from Jessie

If you've picked up this book and it's your very first Jessie title, or if you've (literally) read 100 of my other titles (I think this is book #105 or something) I just wanted to say a special "Thank You" for giving my work and me a few - or more - hours of your time. Time is a precious commodity and I don't take yours lightly.

I love interacting with readers. I do that through my newsletter, where I share stories of farm life and announce sales and new releases and you get a free book just for signing up, through my Facebook group, where more than three thousand of us laugh and pray for each other, and through my Patreon group, where I offer my newest releases for download before they're available on retailers.

I deeply appreciate my readers, whether I chat with you on a regular basis, or whether I don't, and I just wanted to take the time here to say so: Thank you for reading, thank you for your time, thank you for your support, your kind words, your encouragement, your reviews and sharing my stories with your family and friends and requesting my books at your libraries. Without all of you, and your amazing support, I would not be able to continue to write. God is good.

And last, special and heartfelt thanks to my Patreon group! I appreciate your support of my writing and books so very much.

Thanks so much for spending time with me today!

Hugs and love,

Jessie Gussman

JESSIE GUSSMAN

November 6, 2023, Amherst, Virginia

Chapter 1

"Who is the dude standing over there in the corner?" Norma Jean asked Eleanor Landry as they stood by the punch bowl at the first annual Strawberry Sands Christmas barn dance.

Eleanor glanced over the rim of her cup. "That's Peter Slessing. He's the brother of the business partner of my sister's husband, Noah."

"Oh my goodness, you're related to him?" Norma Jean said with her mouth hanging wide open.

Maybe that was a little confusing. She could understand how Norma Jean didn't quite get it. But she didn't know how else to explain him, because Peter wasn't exactly a part of Strawberry Sands.

"He just bought a farm outside of town this year. So, he's kind of new around town."

"I thought you said he was related to you?" Norma Jean slanted him another glance out of the corner of her eye.

Eleanor knew what that look meant a mile away. Norma Jean was interested in the handsome farmer.

Eleanor could understand why. The man was attractive, with his square jaw, the dark stubble on his cheeks, and the cowboy hat that sat low on his forehead. Of course, he was wearing a button-down plaid shirt along with jeans and boots. Eleanor was a sucker for boots.

But Norma Jean was interested, and Eleanor wouldn't have anything to do with a man who someone else had already declared as a love interest, especially when that someone was the cousin of her best friend, Sally.

"He doesn't seem to want to date any of the girls in town though," Eleanor said, wanting Norma Jean to be informed.

"Is this the guy that you were telling me wasn't interested in anyone?"

"Yeah. Different people have approached him, and he's just been kinda standoffish." She was going to stop there, but she thought maybe she should give the man the benefit of the doubt. "My mom says he's just busy getting his farm ready for winter, but..." She looked around the barn. She had been in charge of making sure it was decorated for Christmas, with wreaths hanging up on the doors, twinkle lights hanging from the rafters, and festive ribbons and bows everywhere, along with four different Christmas trees, complete with presents underneath them. Christmas music played out of portable speakers, and there was a jovial, happy atmosphere. She had to say she was pleased with her handiwork.

"Winter has more than descended," she said.

"Maybe I can figure out how to get him to be less standoffish." Norma Jean wiggled her brows.

"Good luck with that. I'm surprised he's even here. Probably Franklin dragged him along with him."

"Franklin?"

"He's a businessman from Chicago and partner to my sister's husband."

"Oh. That's how the family connection comes in."

"Yeah, a connection, but no relation." Eleanor hadn't spent too much time getting to know Franklin. He'd been around, and she knew him to recognize him, but he always seemed preoccupied with whatever it was that he did in Chicago.

Her sister Sunday indicated that he might be moving to Strawberry Sands and in fact had bought property along with Noah, her husband. But Franklin didn't seem as interested in moving to a small town.

Eleanor allowed her eyes to drift over the crowd until she found Franklin standing in the corner. He had been talking to Noah earlier, but she saw Noah following along behind his wife as she led him to the dance floor.

Now Franklin stood by himself, his head down, scrolling on his phone. She got the feeling that he would rather be anywhere other than where he was.

"I'm going to go ask him to dance," Norma Jean said, draining the last of her punch and setting her cup down at the end of one of the picnic tables set up by the refreshment table. "Wish me luck."

Eleanor couldn't get any words out before Norma Jean walked away. She wanted to tell her to come back. For some reason, neither Franklin nor Peter seemed like the marrying type. Or interested in a small-town girl type. Maybe that was more what she meant.

But then, Norma Jean wasn't the kind of person who sat back and allowed life to happen to her. Unlike Eleanor.

Eleanor shifted, not liking the direction her thoughts were going. She didn't want to be the kind of person who life happened to. She wanted to be the kind of person who grabbed life by the horns and fitted it to suit her.

Well, she wanted to do the Lord's will too. But she didn't think God wanted her sitting in a corner, wishing her life was different, rather than going out and making it different.

If you were going to do that, you'd walk over there and ask Franklin to dance with you.

That was true. But she didn't want to. He might say no.

And what's going to happen to you if he says no?

Good question. Nothing. Other than she'd be embarrassed, and the next few times she saw him at any kind of town or family get-together, she'd want to hide in a corner.

Why? What's so terrible about asking someone to dance, having them decline? It doesn't mean anything. You simply found out they weren't interested. It's not like you're going to risk your life or anything.

She didn't like the little voice in her head. Well, she appreciated it, because it was trying to get her out of her corner and into a more active lifestyle.

She knew her mother worried about her, and Eleanor hated to add that extra burden to her. Her mom had been so good to her, and she wanted to return the favor. She knew there were a lot of people who turned their backs on their parents as they got older or, at the very least, shut their parents out of their lives and didn't give them any say in it. She couldn't see any justification for that in the Bible, and indeed, the Bible taught that a child should listen to their parents and absorb the wisdom that was shared. After all, who loved a person more than their mother?

Her mother only wanted the best for her.

But she didn't want to take the risk of rejection.

If you don't change something, you can't expect anything to change.

She wasn't sure exactly what that meant, although it kind of made sense in her head. She couldn't expect her life to go in a different direction if she wasn't willing to do anything different to make it change direction.

All right.

She glanced across the room. Norma Jean had gotten waylaid by Miss Heather. Miss Heather could be quite a force of nature, and as Eleanor watched, Norma Jean started to walk away, but Miss Heather grabbed her arm, pulling her back and continuing to talk.

If you move fast, you could be dancing with Franklin before Norma Jean even gets to Peter.

Eleanor wasn't typically a competitive person, but if she was turning over a new leaf, she might as well turn it over all the way.

Taking her cup and setting it down on the picnic table beside Norma Jean's, she took a breath and decided that she would do something totally out of character. She would walk over to Franklin and ask him to dance.

The barn felt a lot bigger when she was standing on the other side of it, but the walk across seemed short. She found herself praying that Miss Heather would let Norma Jean go and come over and waylay her.

That's silly. You can do this. You're an adult.

Maybe this was why she worked as a dog groomer. She could relate to dogs. They were easy. Hard to offend, pretty happy with anything, and food motivated them.

Unlike people. Who usually weren't happy with anything, were easy to offend—Eleanor seemed to stick her foot in her mouth more times than not—and she still hadn't figured out what motivated most people.

Maybe it was because she'd been rejected so much when she was younger. She just seemed awkward in conversations, always saying something that no one else understood. Her mind went in different directions, while everyone else in the room seemed to be thinking on the same wavelength.

She'd kind of given up ever fitting in anywhere. Which was why she was alone, a dog groomer, and not married like her siblings. Ryan was the only other one who hadn't gotten married, and she could understand why. He'd been busy on the rodeo circuit, going from place to place, never staying in one spot very long. He hadn't had time to settle down.

But now that he was back in Strawberry Sands to stay, she was sure he'd be married before the end of next year.

But her. She was pretty much hopeless. Except, she was turning over that new leaf. It was practically spinning since she was going to go over and ask Franklin to dance. He would say yes, and they would have an engaging conversation while they danced without stepping on each other's toes to a whole big pile of Christmas songs that would become their new playlist after they got married two Christmases from now.

Yeah, and if Franklin had any idea what she was thinking, he would run in the opposite direction as she walked toward him.

She should just take it moment by moment. Live in the moment. Wasn't that the advice that everyone was given?

She'd never been able to do that either. She had her whole life planned out. Of course, nothing had gone as planned, especially after her longtime high school boyfriend, who also happened to be her boyfriend through two years of college, had broken up with her.

And it wasn't just that he had broken up with her; after he walked away, she found out from different people that he'd been cheating on her the entire time they'd been together.

She felt like an idiot. And at the time, she vowed never to have another relationship. But that seemed like a stupid thing to do, she just...hadn't been able to get back in the game. Or maybe she hadn't developed the skills necessary to play the game.

Or maybe there wasn't a game. After all, dating wasn't really necessary, was it? It was a modern thing. Two hundred years ago, people didn't date. Which she could really appreciate at this point in her life.

And with that thought, she was standing in front of Franklin, who didn't look up from his phone.

"Excuse me," Eleanor said, trying to swallow her nervousness, although she couldn't keep from twisting her hands together in front of her.

Franklin finished the text or whatever he was doing before he looked up. He looked around, his eyes widening before they landed back on her.

Franklin might not ever grace the cover of a modeling magazine, and he most likely wouldn't land on bodybuilders.com, but his dark hair was neatly clipped, and his eyes were a rich, deep brown behind the glasses that perched on his nose.

They must be for reading, because he looked at her over them.

"Are you talking to me?" he asked, like she wasn't standing directly in front of him.

"Dance me with you like I mean would." The words came out of her mouth, but even she was confused about what she was trying to say. So it was no surprise when Franklin's brows drew down.

"Again, please? This time in English?"

She wanted to fall through the floor. Had she ever been more embarrassed in her entire life? Probably. She'd done lots of embarrassing things. But she was having trouble remembering anything that was quite this bad.

She needed to apologize for being so confusing.

"My sorry bad dancer you few." That didn't come out right either. Apparently, she combined asking him to dance again with apologizing for messing up her first invitation.

Her brain never could do two things at once, and apparently her mouth was even worse at it.

She was opening her mouth to try to make some sense out of the situation, as Franklin seemed to be genuinely interested in what she was trying to say, or maybe he was just concerned that the insane asylum had had a breakout, when his phone buzzed loudly.

He glanced down, looked at the phone screen for a moment, then looked back up. "I'm sorry. I have to take this."

He swiped on his phone, put it to his ear, and said, "Hello?" as he turned and walked a few steps away from her. Considering they were standing in a corner, he couldn't get far, but that was all it took.

Eleanor considered herself the most inept person in the world, put her tail between her legs, and scurried away.

Chapter 2

Franklin felt bad for not helping the woman who had stood in front of him, but his attention had been completely diverted by his phone call.

"Are you serious?" he said, unpleasant surprise making his stomach feel like it had exploded.

"I'm sorry. I don't have a choice but to fly to Africa tonight. I wish I didn't have to do it, but my sister could die. I need to go see her."

Maisie, a business associate, was on the other end. He didn't work with her much, she didn't work for his company, but they'd come to an agreement after meeting at a business function where both of them had been dateless. They'd agreed that if Maisie needed a date, he would be there for her. And she had agreed to do the same for him.

He hated the Christmas season, because there were so many company functions that he was expected to go to, and he was always expected to have a date.

Maisie wasn't any more interested in him than he was in her, but their arrangement suited each of them, and it had worked out well.

Until now.

"I'm sorry to hear she has malaria," he said, trying to infuse sympathy in his voice. He really did feel bad for Maisie and her sister. Malaria was serious, and people did die from it, although he didn't know anyone personally. But he selfishly wished that she could have gotten malaria after this weekend's charity gala, so he wouldn't have to scramble to try to find a date or go solo.

He could hardly ask Maisie to delay her flight. Of course she wanted to rush to her sister's side.

"Thanks for letting me know," he said, trying not to sound glum and depressed. He could show up without a date. He supposed people had, although it usually didn't happen. It was the kind of place where it was nice to have someone at his side, and he would stick out like a sore thumb if he didn't.

If he didn't sit on the board of directors for that particular charity, he would weasel his way out of it. But he could hardly do that. He was in charge of the silent auction for the evening, and he had assumed his date was going to be helping him. Maisie always did.

The charity benefited a local Chicago dog shelter, and it was very popular. It was always a point of pride with his company on how much money was raised. That was why he handled the auction himself.

"I can hit up a couple of my friends and see if any of them would be able to go with you. But I can't do it right now. I'm actually on hold with the airline. They're trying to get me bumped up to an earlier flight. I need to go."

"Sure. Thanks."

She murmured something else, and then he swiped his phone off.

He didn't know what he was going to do, but he did know that he wasn't going to be able to fix the problem right now. Maybe one of her friends would come through for her. And maybe he could figure something out. But in the meantime, these people had planned this party partly because of the hotel he and his partner, Noah, had built. And while he had to respond to a few urgent inquiries earlier, he wanted to do his best to mingle with the people in town, show his appreciation, and enjoy it. So far, the hotel was a smashing success, and he was grateful to Strawberry Sands for all their wonderful support.

Franklin looked around, trying to find the woman who had come over and been speaking gibberish to him. He'd been grateful for the call, because he had no idea of how to handle that.

It wasn't that he was suave and sophisticated. Far from it. And he'd grown up in Strawberry Sands, so he wasn't exactly a big-city guy, although he enjoyed living in Chicago. It was just...he was much happier with his head buried in numbers, talking business, strategy, sales projections, and that type of thing. He would rather talk about inflation or taxes than have some woman, who was quite pretty, standing in front of him leaving him speechless.

He looked around again and saw her standing over beside the punch table, guzzling a drink.

He actually kind of liked her a little. But he didn't feel that it was right for him to come into Strawberry Sands and start dating the local girls. Especially when he had no intention of leaving Chicago permanently. And from his experience, most of the time girls who lived in small towns didn't want to go to the big city to raise a family.

Although he had bought ground in the area and had gotten all the approvals and paperwork done that he needed in order to start building, he hadn't yet broken ground.

Maybe that was because he hadn't yet decided whether or not he actually wanted to move to Strawberry Sands.

Noah had fallen in love, and that had made his decision easy.

But for Franklin, he missed the excitement of the big city. The noise, the convenience, and the feeling that he was never alone.

Sometimes Strawberry Sands could feel lonely.

Maybe that was just because of the fact that when he was here, he was more aware than at any other time that he was over thirty and didn't have any family around him at all. He was practically married to his business.

And he knew that wasn't healthy.

Except, he loved what he did. Loved the challenge and the excitement and the rush of success. He even loved when things weren't going well, loved trying to see what he could do to fix everything and turn it all around.

Of course, he hadn't had to do that for a long time, since their businesses had been going well.

The hotel that Noah and he had built in Strawberry Sands was open and thriving. Even in the winter, which they hadn't expected.

But Strawberry Sands had thrown in behind them. Case in point, tonight. The first annual Strawberry Sands Christmas barn dance.

The people of Strawberry Sands had spent months planning it and had advertised everywhere.

They couldn't have had a better turnout. And it seemed like people were having fun.

Everyone but him, who had been accosted by someone who had either had too much alcohol before she arrived or had some kind of issue he wasn't able to help her fix.

Too bad, because Eleanor had seemed like a nice girl. She was the sister of the woman Noah had married.

"Hey, bro. Why aren't you on the dance floor?" His brother, Peter, came up beside him, clapping a hand on his shoulder.

"You know I can't dance." Not only did he have two left feet, he had no sense of the beat, and he knew none of the songs that were playing. Well, he knew some of the Christmas songs, but normally, whatever was playing, he had no clue. He listened to classical music, which was a drag for most girls. So it wasn't something that he led with. In fact, he never had a relationship that had gotten to the point where he'd ever had to confess it.

Peter laughed, then he grew serious and leaned closer. "You know, what you need is a hat. Chicks dig it."

Franklin laughed and shook his head. A hat wouldn't go well with his glasses, and there was no way he was taking them off. He couldn't see a thing without them.

Peter had perfect vision and was the least serious of the two of them. That wasn't saying much, considering Franklin was serious and driven, but the last year had been hard and it was good to see his brother smiling.

"Want some punch?" Peter asked, holding a glass up.

The music had switched to something jazzy and upbeat, and couples swirled around the floor. It must have been a really popular song, because the dance floor swelled as people jumped and swayed to the music.

Franklin reached out to grab the glass, but as he did so, someone jostled Peter, and he lurched forward, the red juice going down the front of Franklin's white shirt.

It wasn't Peter's fault, and it wasn't really the fault of the person who jostled him, who had turned around and was apologizing profusely.

"It's okay." Franklin put his hand up. "You didn't see him."

"Sorry, bro," Peter said, looking at the red stain that had soaked into the entire front of Franklin's shirt.

"It's okay. I mean, I like red," he added lamely. He was just as upset that he was wet as he was that his shirt was stained.

The folks on the floor moved away, resuming their dance, as Peter stared at the front of Franklin's shirt.

"I've got a spare in my pickup. It's not the kind you usually wear, but it'll work." He grinned. "And to show my sincerest apologies, you can have my hat." He grabbed his cowboy hat that was perched on his head and plopped it down on top of Franklin's.

Normally, Franklin would grab it and throw it back at him, but he was more concerned about getting to the bathroom and getting the wet shirt off than he was about shoving Peter's hat back at him.

"Actually, here. You take this one, and I'll just throw my other one on while I'm standing at the pickup." The restrooms were just down the hall a few feet from where they stood. As was the door to the outside.

That made the most sense to Franklin, and he didn't argue as Peter unbuttoned his shirt, balled it up, and shoved it at him.

They'd always been pretty much the same size. As long as he left the top button open, it wouldn't matter much.

"Go on. Go change. I owe you one."

"Thanks," Franklin said, taking the shirt and walking to the bathroom.

He might as well throw his white shirt in the garbage can. That red punch would never come out. It would just give his dry cleaner fits.

So far, it hadn't been a very good night. He'd been approached by someone who was either high or drunk, had lost his date for the weekend, had his shirt ruined, and ended up wearing his brother's clothes.

He laughed. At least he knew that the night could not possibly get any worse.

Chapter 3

"That is a terrible idea," Eleanor said, trying to be the voice of reason. Sally, her best friend, was several years younger than she was, and she hardly ever noticed the age difference. Except today, it seemed like Sally had reverted back to being a teenager, and Eleanor felt like her grandmother.

"It's a perfect idea. Peter couldn't dance because he had just gotten punch for his brother. But he's a farmer, so he loves animals, and if I can just get him and Norma Jean alone together, I know they'd hit it off."

Sally had somehow overheard a brief exchange between Peter and her cousin and had immediately started plotting on how she could get the two of them alone without any distractions like brothers or punch. She always had some kind of plan up her sleeve, and usually it was to help people. As this purportedly was. However, Eleanor had her doubts about this one.

"Kidnapping someone is a felony." She had no idea what kind of crime it was. She just knew that a person couldn't kidnap someone and think it was okay.

"I'm not kidnapping anyone. I'm simply going to talk him into seeing something with me, and then once we've done that, I'll leave him there and have Norma Jean come save him. There's a storm coming tonight, and they might possibly get snowed in together, which is perfect. This is the perfect storm."

Wasn't there a book with that name? Eleanor got sidetracked for just a moment as she had a tendency to do. Her brain just went in different directions, and no one ever really understood how she managed to connect the things she did. But it made perfect sense to her.

By the time she came back to focusing on what was going on in front of her, Sally was knee-deep in her plan.

"There's a mama cat with baby kittens, and I'll just have him come help me with them. I'll say that she's having trouble delivering or something."

"So there's no mother?"

"There is. She's just not in distress. Not that I know of anyway."

"And there are kittens?"

"There's going to be kittens. Someday." Sally had a pleading look on her face. "Please. I've been taking care of Wilma for the past six months, and I've barely gotten out. At all. In fact, this is the first fun thing that I've done, aside from going to the pharmacy and picking up Depends, in months. Please. We'll leave tonight, knowing we did a good deed for Norma Jean, plus, having fun ourselves, and not keep feeling like the rest of the world has passed us by, along with all the fun everyone else is having."

"I don't feel like that," Eleanor said. Although she did feel bad for Sally. She really had been taking care of her Aunt Wilma who had been bedridden since her stroke.

Eleanor felt guilty that she hadn't helped Sally more. A caretaker's job was an extremely difficult one, and Sally hardly ever complained.

Eleanor hated to turn her down for this one small request.

Actually, kidnapping a grown man was a rather big request. But still... She sighed. Was this just a part of her never-wanting-to-do-anything-fun personality? Wasn't she just thinking earlier that she needed to turn over a new leaf?

Of course, that hadn't worked out very well for her. The new leaf that she turned over had gotten smashed underneath Franklin's foot.

She lifted her eyes to where he had been standing in the corner. He was gone.

And it was just as well. She hadn't been able to get her words out properly, which she still wanted to crawl under the table about, but he hadn't been very polite either, answering the phone in the middle of their conversation, such as it was, since she hadn't been able to actually say anything coherent, and then turning away from her with a wave of his hand.

She wanted to be mad at him, but she knew she was the one to blame. She, who couldn't get her tongue to work when it needed to.

She could hardly blame him.

"All right. Here's the plan, we're going to get Peter to go to a shed on the far side of his property. Remember we used to play there when we were kids?"

"I remember. But I still think this isn't a good idea."

"Listen, they can't say that we're kidnapping him if we take him to his own property, right?"

"I guess," Eleanor said, wishing she could think of an excuse not to help. She had a very bad feeling about this.

"Eleanor!"

Eleanor almost sighed in relief as she heard Sunday calling her.

She turned, with maybe a bigger smile on her face than absolutely necessary. "Sunday! How are you enjoying your first barn dance?"

"I'm having a great time," Sunday said, but she nodded her head across the floor. "But Ryan has been stuck in a corner all night. I wish I could think of a way to get him out." Sunday looked over at Sally. "Do you think you might go ask him to dance?"

"I'm sorry. I'm busy. But maybe later, after I get this…thing done that I need to do." She gave Eleanor a look that Eleanor interpreted easily. She wasn't to breathe a word about what Sally was about to do.

Sally didn't have to worry about that. Eleanor didn't want to have anything to do with it at all. Nothing.

In fact, she was so eager to get away that she almost offered to dance with her brother herself. Unfortunately, that would only embarrass both of them. So she walked off with Sunday as they tried to brainstorm a way to get Ryan out of his corner and enjoying life in Strawberry Sands. It was obvious that he missed the rodeo, or…maybe there was someone on the rodeo circuit he missed.

Eleanor tucked that information in the back of her head and followed her sister. Maybe she could do a little digging and see if there might be something she could do to help Ryan, something that didn't involve kidnapping anyone.

Chapter 4

"She's having so much trouble having her kittens, and I just needed you to help me. I knew that you could do it. Since you're a farmer." Sally knew she sounded ridiculous, but she blinked her big blue eyes up at Peter, hoping that he would fall to her charm—the charm of her blue eyes and blonde hair and the innocent, childish expression that she often was told she had.

It wasn't that she was a terrible, calculating person. It was just that once a person had been told that they look so sweet and innocent so many times, they started to believe it. Or maybe...they figured out a way to use it to their benefit, instead of always being annoyed about it.

She was almost thirty. But she was still being mistaken for an eighteen-year-old and had just been carded when she tried to buy cough syrup for goodness' sake. And the last time she tried to buy a pocketknife, she'd been denied permission, because she forgot her purse and couldn't produce her driver's license.

It was annoying.

Except for now, when hopefully her baby blues were doing what they were supposed to do.

Peter looked down at her from underneath his cowboy hat. His blue button-down contrasted nicely with the dark brown of his eyes. She hadn't seen too many people wear a cowboy hat and glasses at the same time, but Peter pulled the look off.

"So I put on a cowboy hat, and everybody thinks I know everything there is to know about animals?"

"Please. I don't want to bother anyone else. Strawberry Sands doesn't have too many fun times, and this is the biggest thing that's ever happened in our town. I hate to drag anyone else off. But..."

"I was standing in the corner and didn't look like I had anything else better to do?" Peter finished her sentence for her when she paused.

She wasn't going to put it quite like that. Honestly, that wasn't exactly what she was thinking. She was thinking more along the lines of that it had turned out her cousin had a huge crush on him, and she thought they could really hit it off if they spent time together. So she was going to kidnap him and trap him in a shed with her cousin so they could have the opportunity to get to know each other.

But she just did her best imitation of a simper and nodded, blinking her best features again and trying to look at him like she admired him and knew that he could do it.

She heard from somewhere that men were suckers when a person thought they could help.

But Peter didn't seem too eager to run off with her.

"Please? We're supposed to get a really bad snowstorm, and I'm afraid she'll die if we don't take care of her now."

There was a cat in the shed, and it was pregnant. She hadn't wanted to lie, so she'd borrowed the cat that they'd found living in the barn when they'd cleaned it up in preparation for the dance. She was just stretching the truth since it wasn't in labor. Stretching it out of shape, for the most part.

But she tried to push that aside. She was doing a good deed for her cousin.

"I guess I might as well. Even if I really have no clue of what I'm doing."

"Don't farmers deal with animals all the time?" she asked, blinking again and grabbing onto his arm as he pushed off from the wall. She didn't want to lose him. Thankfully, they were close to the back door, and she guided him that way.

"I'm not—"

"Careful," she said as she skipped out of the way of an unruly dancer. Really, the community should have dances more often. The folks in Strawberry Sands were so out of practice that they got a little wild with their dance moves.

He put his hand on her back, and she appreciated how he steadied her, but she skipped away as soon as she could. She didn't really like people touching her, especially strangers. It was true that she was doing this for her cousin, but it was probably also true that someone ought to stage an intervention for her. She was pretty hopeless.

But not tonight. Tonight was all about Norma Jean finally finding the man of her dreams. She'd always wanted a cowboy, and this cowboy came complete with hat, boots, and that plaid button-down shirt that made her cousin's heart flutter like a butterfly's wings.

It didn't do much for Sally, but that was fine, since this wasn't her guy.

"My car is right here," she said, guiding him to the closest space in the parking lot. She managed to snag it when the old ladies who stayed with Kristin and her husband had left early.

Sally had been looking for such an opening and had grabbed her car and moved it to that spot immediately.

She was glad she'd taken the time, because she wasn't sure whether she would get Peter to walk the whole way across the parking lot or not. He seemed very reluctant.

"How far away did you say the shed was?" he asked again as she guided him to the passenger door and opened it for him. He didn't duck down to sit.

"It's on your farm. Right at the edge. Eleanor and I used to play in it when we were little."

For some reason, when she mentioned Eleanor's name, the man's eyes twitched. Maybe it was because he knew her through his brother being business partners with Eleanor's sister's husband.

That connection was rather dubious, and it took a little bit for Sally to wrap her head around it all.

But that was the way small towns were. Everybody was related to, or at least knew, everybody else.

After another moment's hesitation, he ducked his head and sat down in the car.

She breathed a sigh of relief. Now, all she had to do was lock him in the back room of the shed.

It was more like a cabin.

There was a woodstove, and she'd made sure that there was plenty of wood there. Just in case her plan came to fruition. She'd also dropped off a care package with romantic things like candles, matches, and two blankets. She'd thought about only providing one, so they'd be forced to share, but finally decided on two because she didn't want to be liable if they didn't get along and one of them froze to death. She'd also provided drinks and food.

She hurried around the front of the car and tried to keep up a stream of steady chatter the whole way to the cabin. It was a fifteen-minute drive that she tried to make in less than ten minutes. She was afraid that he would realize how ridiculous it was for her to be asking about a cat she couldn't possibly have checked on for hours.

She thought he was probably getting suspicious by the end of their trip, so she blinked her eyes at him again.

"All right. We're here!" she said cheerfully, then remembered that she was supposed to be worried. "I hope Fluff, er, Fluffers is okay." She hadn't thought to name the cat. Well, she just did.

The man sighed, checked his phone again, and then he followed her lead as she opened her door and got out.

"This will only take a minute. I'm sure of it. Fluffers has always been a good mother and had easy deliveries of her babies."

She needed to shut her mouth. She was saying the stupidest things.

"I see. I mean, I—"

"All right. Come on in. If you don't mind, can I use your phone flashlight, since there's no electricity here?" This was a long shot, but if she could get him to give her his phone, she'd have a better chance of him not getting anyone to come help him get out. She felt some guilt but reasoned in her heart that it was for a good cause, and he'd thank her on his and Norma Jean's wedding day.

"My phone flashlight?" the man muttered, pulling it back out of his pocket and turning the flashlight on. He handed it to her, and she shined it around the cabin, hiding her satisfied smile.

The cabin was dusty and small. But there was a woodstove, and just because she thought he was going to need it, she said, "I've always loved this cabin, and it has such a big pile of wood stacked outside the back door."

There. Now he knew there was wood outside the back door. So when Norma Jean showed up and the storm trapped them together, they would be able to make a nice, cozy fire. Relationships thrived in front of the natural warmth of a beautiful flame.

"Fluffers is in here." She did call her Fluffers, right?

But Peter didn't seem to notice anything amiss, so she hurried to the back where the storage closet was.

"Right in here," she said, holding her breath. This was the trickiest part. He needed to be far enough in that she could close the door and lock it before he had the foresight, no, the *inclination* to turn around and try to open the door. He was much bigger than she was, and she would never be able to hold it closed without getting it locked.

"This seems like an odd place for a cat. How'd she get in?" Peter said, looking around.

"You know cats. They can get in anywhere." She knew no such thing, and Peter didn't seem to either, because he gave her a look underneath the cowboy hat as the phone flashlight glowed a little on his face. His eyes were dark and unreadable, and Sally felt a shiver go down her back. Not a good one. This man was not a man she wanted to have anything to do with. He felt a little dangerous. Definitely more serious than what she was interested in.

Thankfully, just then they heard a meow, and the man tilted his head.

"She sounds like she's in distress!" Sally said, although she wouldn't have said any such thing. It sounded like a curious meow, like the cat was wondering when someone was going to come and let her out.

Peter opened the door, and she reached to shine the flashlight in. Thankfully, Fluffers was over on the pile of towels that Sally had placed in the corner.

One step. Two. Three.

Sally slammed the door closed and threw the lock, just as her phone buzzed in her pocket.

She pulled it out, shoving Peter's phone in her opposite pocket, and looked down.

The text appeared in front of her eyes as Peter called through the door, "Hey! What are you doing?"

The text was from Norma Jean.

> **Sally! Forget about your plan! Peter just looked me up and he wanted to dance! I don't think you're going to have to kidnap him after all!**

Sally's jaw dropped, and she barely noticed four exclamation points in one text. She stared at her phone some more. Norma Jean was with Peter?

The man in the closet pounded on the door. "This isn't a very good joke. Let me out."

His voice sounded commanding and irritated.

Sally, who had never been very brave to begin with and who had a physically abusive father who became violent when he was angry, swallowed past her suddenly tight throat. She'd made a huge mistake.

"Peter?"

"And for the last time and for goodness' sake, stop calling me Peter. That's my brother."

Sally's eyes grew big, and her hand went to her heart.

She had screwed up. Big time.

Her fingers shook, but she sent a text to the one person she knew she could always count on. Her best friend, Eleanor.

> I've kidnapped the wrong man.

Chapter 5

Eleanor looked around the dance floor. People were having a great time, the lights sparkled, Christmas music poured from hidden speakers, people were smiling and laughing, and the atmosphere was just perfect.

She would have thought it couldn't have gotten better and would have bet that nothing could ruin the evening.

But she would have been wrong.

Sally had gone ahead with her crazy plan, and not only gone ahead with it, but had kidnapped the wrong man.

If that wasn't bad enough, she panicked and was even now driving back to the barn dance, leaving the man locked in the back room of the shed.

She'd stopped answering Eleanor's texts, so Eleanor assumed she was driving.

Her last text said she was scared to open the door because she was afraid the man would get mad at her and hurt her, even though Franklin had never been violent with anyone that Eleanor knew of.

Sally had grown up with an abusive father, so it made sense to Eleanor that she was scared.

It didn't make sense to her that she had driven away from the cabin completely though.

Surely she could stay and at least keep the man company until Eleanor managed to get there.

She finally found her mother in the crowd and walked toward her, focused and thankful that no one tried to stop her to chat.

"I need to leave for a bit, Mom."

Her mom, standing behind the raffle table where everyone was buying tickets for the big Christmas cookie tray giveaway, where proceeds went to the Blueberry Beach humane society, looked up in surprise.

"You're leaving? Are you okay? Are you sick?" Her mom poured the questions out, the way a seasoned mother would do, her brow furrowed in concern, knowing that Eleanor had put a lot of work into making the barn dance a success and wouldn't be leaving for a small reason.

"I just have something I need to do. I probably won't be gone long, but don't worry about me. I can't really tell you what's going on, it has to do with Sally."

Her mother's lips formed an "O," and she started nodding in understanding. Sally had created more than a few issues Eleanor had had to straighten out over the years.

"All right. But I want a full report as soon as you're able to say."

She smiled and nodded at her mom. Her mom understood the value of friends and the importance of keeping a confidence. She appreciated that, that and the fact that her mom didn't try to micromanage her life, as tempting as it probably was. She was almost thirty and hadn't gotten married, didn't have any prospects, and was totally content with her small dog grooming business. She wasn't super happy about her lack of romance, and her mom knew it. She probably wanted to try to matchmake. But she refrained.

At least as far as Eleanor knew.

With that thought, she hurried out of the barn, hearing the waves of Lake Michigan crashing in the distance and smelling the scent of horses on the wind.

It was cold, and a storm was brewing, would be there any time. In fact, as she hurried to her car through the parking lot, the first snowflakes were dribbling down.

The barn dance would soon be breaking up, and people would be going home. No one wanted to drive in the kind of snow that they were supposed to get. High winds, low visibility, and snow totals reaching up to two feet. It would be tomorrow afternoon before the snow stopped, and probably the next day before most roads were plowed out.

Everyone was probably planning on staying home tomorrow if they possibly could. Even though they lived in Michigan and were used to this kind of weather, snow was always more enjoyable when one wasn't trying to drive in it.

She pulled out on the road, but an orange glow made her look down.

Shoot. With all the dance preparations, she'd forgotten to get gas. Her car was almost out.

Then she remembered the last time her light had come on, it had barely been another twenty miles before she'd been sitting along the road.

Thankfully, Peter's farm wasn't that far away, and she should be able to get Franklin out fairly quickly.

Regardless, it made a curl of anxiety go through her, and what had been just a routine *save the dude who was kidnapped from the shed and bring him back to the party, soothing his ruffled feathers and making sure he wasn't going to sue anybody* had turned into a *hope she wasn't stranded along the road in the middle of a snowstorm out of gas.*

That probably wouldn't be worse than being sued in the long run, but in the short run, she couldn't think of too many things that she would not want more.

This was probably going to be about the most awkward thing in the world, since she'd just asked the dude to dance, only hadn't done it in a coherent manner, and not only had he not understood what she was asking, but she'd scared him away.

Sure, he'd gotten a phone call, but still, he had made no effort to continue to talk to her.

Not that she could blame him.

Pulling off the road with a cautious eye on her gas gauge, which showed she was less than empty, she pulled down the mostly grass drive toward the shed. Maybe once upon a time, it had been well used on the farm, but until Peter had bought the farm earlier that year, it had been pretty much abandoned.

There wasn't even a house on the farm anymore. It had fallen into disrepair and been bulldozed by the previous owner.

As far as she knew, Peter was living with his brother in Strawberry Sands over the old diner.

There'd been rumors around town that both of them were planning on building houses near Strawberry Sands, but if they had, she hadn't heard about it.

Knowing that this was going to be one of the most awkward and embarrassing things that she'd ever endured in her life before, after the unfortunate encounter at the dance where her words wouldn't work, Eleanor put her car in park and held onto the wheel for just a moment staring at the shed.

If this were her...would she be upset?

She'd probably be scared, to be honest. She was pretty sure that Franklin had been in town long enough to know that no one meant any harm by it. And he wasn't in any danger. No one could look at Sally and think she could harm a fly. But if it were her, she'd be afraid that she was going to be stuck in the room forever. She didn't particularly like to be alone and in the dark.

She couldn't figure out whether she would be upset or not. Sometimes when she got scared, she covered it with anger. Not on purpose, that just seemed to be something she did naturally.

Regardless, she couldn't blame him for being angry. Just because something didn't upset her didn't mean it shouldn't upset someone else. The man had been taken from a dance under false pretenses and shoved in a closet, out in the middle of nowhere, well, on his brother's farm, but still. And then he'd been abandoned.

Hopefully he wasn't a violent type of person, and suddenly with that thought, Eleanor thought maybe Sally was smart for not opening the door and letting him out. She was a little afraid that if he had a tendency toward violence, he wouldn't be able to control himself.

She would say she deserved it, but while she knew her friend had been thinking about this, she hadn't thought she'd actually go through with it.

Trying not to think about all the people she knew who would be very upset, very angry, over this, she reached for the door latch and got out of her car. Whatever Franklin felt, she would have to face it. She would have to take the blame, even if she didn't feel like it was entirely her fault. Because nothing was his fault.

He had thought he was doing a good deed by helping someone with a cat in distress, and instead, he ended up trapped.

Looking around at the snow that was falling steadily and thick, with occasional gusts of wind, she figured she needed to hurry, or she really wasn't going to be able to drive home.

Her tires were mostly bald; she'd been waiting until winter to put new ones on. Then, with all the preparations for the barn dance, she hadn't had time.

She shoved those thoughts aside; she'd figure out how to get home, after she rescued Franklin.

There were no lights on in the small cabin, if anyone could call it that. She knew there was a small woodstove, but she didn't know whether there was anything else. Including food.

In all of her ramblings, Sally hadn't mentioned whether they'd left food for the couple, only that she'd left some sort of "romantic care package," whatever that meant. Surely it would be much more romantic for Sally to trap people inside if they weren't starving to death and tempted to eat each other.

She shivered, thinking of the Donner party.

The snow wasn't going to be Donner party bad, and she had her phone, if they did get stuck. Except...she froze. She'd been using her phone a good bit as she worked to get everything ready for the dance this evening and...she looked down. Yeah. It was on seven percent. Not good.

Of course, everyone would be cleaning up after the barn dance, and she hated to interrupt them, anyway. Especially since she wasn't there to help.

She sighed and started walking toward the door again, smiling at the snow, despite her problems that just seemed to keep piling up. She loved snow, even if it was making her night more difficult.

Weeds grew, dead and dry, on both sides of the path, and she was grateful that it was cold. If it were summer, she'd be concerned about snakes and other critters nesting in the house.

But all of those things should be hibernating right now. Along with her, she thought as she moved her tired body to the door. She'd worked nonstop since she'd gotten up that morning, and the last few days had been chaotic and filled to the brim with work, even though it was a labor of love.

Her back hurt, her ankles hurt, and her stomach growled. She should have eaten more at the dance.

Twisting the knob, she stuck her head in and looked around. It was dark, and she couldn't see much of anything.

"Anyone here?" she said, wondering if she had been the one that had been set up. It did seem a little odd that Sally had slammed the door shut and run away, now that she thought about it. Even though Sally had grown up in an abusive home.

"Back here," a male voice said, with confidence and command in the tone.

It came from the back corner where she knew there was a small room. Maybe that was the door Sally was talking about.

Back when they were kids, they played in the shed, so she had an idea of what it was like, but her memories were fuzzy. They'd spent more than a few hours hiding in the tall weeds and pretending the cabin was their house.

Good memories.

Although most of her childhood had been spent at the lake, this had been a favorite spot when they were old enough to start riding bikes and could get a little farther away from town.

"I'm sorry," she said as she hurried over to the door, using her hands to feel to make sure she didn't run into anything. "I'm sorry that you're locked in here."

"You came back?" He sounded confused.

"No. I'm not Sally. I'm...Eleanor. I...spoke to you a little earlier this evening." She might as well get that out of the way. It would be easier to do before she was face-to-face with him.

"You're the one who didn't make any sense?" The man still sounded a little confused, but now there was a bit of humor in his tone as well.

"Yeah. That was me in all my social awkwardness." She might as well own it. It was the truth.

"Hmm."

He didn't say anything more, and she pulled up the bolt on the latch. It was one of those latches that had a horseshoe-type metal piece sticking out and a metal latch that went over it with a rectangular hole for the horseshoe to fit in, and then a bolt went down through to keep the metal piece there.

She couldn't believe the bolt hadn't gotten lost over the years. But it fit perfectly and slipped right out as she pulled it. Grabbing the metal latch, she pulled that carefully over the U-shaped metal and then used it to pull on the door.

The door didn't move.

She yanked a little harder, wrapping her fingers around the latch and getting a better grip.

Still nothing.

"Umm, I know this isn't what you want to hear, but the door's stuck."

"No, that's really not what I want to hear. Also, there is a cat in here, and she's actually having babies. And I do think she's having issues."

"Can't you see?"

"No. Sally borrowed my phone to use as a flashlight, and when she ran back out, she took it with her."

"Oh. I guess I better conserve the batteries on mine. It's down to 7%." And that was before she'd just used it for the last five minutes.

She turned her phone off as she spoke, wishing she had not been so busy all day and had thought to plug her phone in. Even an hour would have made a difference.

"Who lets their phone get down to seven percent?"

"I know. I was busy doing the barn dance stuff. Decorating and I even did some baking this morning, and I arranged a lot of things, and I also had to watch a few YouTube videos because I couldn't get the icing just right on my cake—" She closed her mouth. There was no point in trying to explain it.

"I forgot. So you're the one who organized that?"

"There were a lot of people involved, but I guess I kind of was in charge."

She was in charge because no one else wanted the job. Or, she should say more fairly, no one else had time.

"How did you get that honor?" he asked, and the humor was back in his voice. He didn't seem terribly upset.

She tugged harder on the door as she spoke. "I guess I just had time. Maybe because I'm not married and don't have kids. And I wanted to, really. I love Strawberry Sands, and the idea of a barn dance was super fun."

She still couldn't get it to move. The door was just not budging.

"Do you think you can push from that side? I mean, I don't want you to worry about stepping on the cat, wherever she is."

"There are some rags or something over in the corner, and that's where she was. That's where I hear her meowing. Is it normal for a cat to meow while she's having babies?"

"I'm not sure." She bit her lip. She did work with animals for a living, but mostly dogs and never while they were having babies. If he had a question about how to clip a dog or what the best shampoo to use was or which brush would fluff hair the best, she could give him some advice.

"I suppose if we get the door open, you can come in and use your phone flashlight to see what's going on. Maybe it's completely normal."

"Yeah," she said, remembering that her phone was at seven percent, and they wouldn't have much time to use the flashlight at all.

She didn't remind him.

"I'm pretty sure the door comes this way. I mean, that makes sense, right?" Surely she hadn't been trying to pull the door when she was supposed to push it.

"Yeah, I think so. It latches on that side, so that would make sense."

He sounded like he was thinking about it, and Eleanor figured as a businessman, Franklin wouldn't have had much opportunity to open doors like this one.

She shivered. She hadn't realized how cold it was. At the barn dance, she'd been active the whole time, bustling around, trying to make sure everything worked just fine. She'd taken a few minutes to rest, mostly when she'd been talking to Sally, and the one time when she went over to ask Franklin to dance with her. Otherwise, she'd been busy most of the night.

Now that she was standing around, the cold was starting to get to her. Her fingers felt it the most, but the rest of her shivered.

"I don't want to smash the door into you," he said, and it sounded like he had come even closer. Maybe was leaning his head down, fiddling with the latch. His voice was just right there.

"I can move back if you want me to."

"How about you do that."

She let go of the latch and moved back and to the side, so when the door opened, she would be well away from it. And from him, in case he came crashing through.

"All right. I'm ready."

There was a thump, and she assumed it was his body hitting the door.

"It didn't budge," he mumbled, and he sounded surprised.

Eleanor couldn't help smiling a little to herself. She didn't feel quite so bad if he couldn't even get the door open. If he had opened it on the first try, she would have felt like she was being inept or something.

Another thump, and still the door did not open. Another, and another.

Finally, he said, "What did she do to it?" He sounded out of breath.

"She didn't tell me that she did anything special. She just said she was afraid to open it because... Well, Sally had an abusive father, and when she does something that she knows is going to make people mad, sometimes she panics. It's just maybe PTSD?"

"I didn't know that," he said, and she realized that there had been a thread of anger in his words, but that sentence sounded contrite, like he felt bad for Sally. She loved what that said about him. About his compassion and his concern for others. It was gratifying to know that he didn't hold it against Sally and maybe even understood.

"I wasn't saying that to try to gain your sympathies. It's the truth. Maybe she shouldn't lock people in rooms if she's afraid of their anger after she does so, but if it makes you feel any better, she didn't mean to lock you in."

"I know. She sounded really surprised when she found out that I wasn't Peter."

"She said something about a cowboy hat and the same color shirt, when she was messaging me," Eleanor said, taking a step closer to the door.

"It's kind of a long story, but basically Peter spilt his drink on me, and that's how I ended up with the shirt."

"And the hat?"

Franklin cleared his throat, and he seemed a little embarrassed, although that was just Eleanor guessing. It was dark and there was a door between them, so maybe she guessed wrong.

"He stuck it on my head and said chicks dig it. I just hadn't had a chance to get it off."

"Oh?" And now she was the one laughing. "Chicks dig the hat? Interesting."

"You ought to know. That's your gender."

"Well, chicks could be male or female, technically. If we're talking about chickens."

"You mean both male and female baby chickens are called chicks," he clarified.

"That is true."

Just then a keening meow split the air, and they both fell silent.

"She was doing that a lot before you came."

"That sounded...not good."

There was another thump as he hit the door again, but it still didn't budge.

"I wonder if we lift it up some, if that would help," Eleanor said thoughtfully. "I seem to remember there being some kind of trick to it." She hadn't really thought about it, but back when they played together, there had been several times, now that she thought about it, when the door had gotten stuck. She'd been trapped in there once with three or four other people, and she'd been too young and dumb to be scared. She just thought it was fun. But as she thought about it, she remembered.

"I'm pretty sure if we lift up on it and pull out at the same time, it gives it a better angle or something. Maybe the hinges sag."

"That would make sense," Franklin said. "Do you remember if there was any kind of slot to put your fingers in, in order to lift up?"

She seemed to remember sticking her fingers underneath the door, where there was a small crack. But...there was also a spot on his side of the door.

"All right. We can lift up underneath the door, but as I recall the crack is pretty small, and my fingers are bigger now than they were then."

"I can feel it, but I can't really get my fingers underneath it." His voice came from down below, like he'd knelt down.

"There is a spot, right underneath the door latch on your side. Be careful running your fingers down, because as I recall, I've gotten more than one splinter from the wood."

"Ouch. You could have said that just a few seconds earlier."

"Sorry."

"It's just common sense. I should have known."

"Kind of tap it with your fingers, don't drag them."

"I think I found it. Yeah, I can get two fingers in."

"All right. You hold onto that, I'll grab the latch on this side, and maybe we can lift up."

She stepped toward the door, putting her hand on the latch and then saying, "I've got mine. Are you ready?"

"Sure. What are we gonna do, on the count of three?"

"Yeah. And I don't think you need to push quite as hard as you were. I'm pretty sure it will slip right out, as long as we lift up the right way."

"All right. You don't want me ramming the door into your face. Got it."

"Well, that's true too."

They shared a little laughter, and then she said, "One, two, three!" She lifted up and then pulled toward her.

She assumed he did the same on the other side, only pushed, and just like she remembered, the door slipped right open.

And she was face-to-face with Franklin Slessing.

Chapter 6

Franklin pulled up just in time to keep from running into Eleanor.

He couldn't see her very well in the dark, but her eyes seemed to be big as she stared at him. They were both breathing hard.

He should have been more irritated. Being taken away from the barn dance, led on some false pretenses that there was a cat who needed help… But he felt like an idiot. Because he never should have fallen for that. It was the dumbest ruse in the book, and if he had been in Chicago, he wouldn't have given it a second thought; he would have turned Sally down flat.

If he would have managed to correct her the first time she called him Peter, none of it would have happened, either.

He wasn't blaming himself. Sally should be held accountable, but he was enough to blame that he just couldn't be angry.

It felt like harmless fun.

Except, he was cold, and there really was a cat who needed help. Or at least it sounded like it.

Another long, painful meow, a sound that made him want to run to the corner and help the poor cat, split the air, and he backed up a step.

"Wow. It's much louder with the door open," Eleanor said, still a little out of breath.

"Do you have your phone?"

She got it out without saying anything, switched the flashlight on, and he led her to the corner.

She knelt down, and he slid over a little so she could have an unobscured view. Out of the two of them, he was assuming she had more experience in cats who were giving birth.

"Wow. That's a huge kitten." Her voice was low and soft. As he looked, he could see that a kitten's head was partially out, but the rest of the body seemed to be stuck.

And even though this kitten was still wet with its fur smashed to its head, it was much, much bigger than the other kitten that had already been born and was dry and puffy, nosing around its mama's belly for its first meal.

"No wonder she's howling so much."

She had barely said that when the cat let out another low, keening cry. She got up, shifting like she was uncomfortable, trying to bend around to lick the kitten that was partially out.

"Is it safe to pull kittens?" he asked.

"I have no idea. But it kind of feels like we need to. I'm not sure she can have it on her own." Eleanor's voice was filled with concern as she reached her hand out to put a finger on the head of the cat.

The cat must have been semi-tame, at least, or else she was in so much distress that she didn't care. Franklin thought touching her was rather brave of Eleanor.

"Do you know this cat?" he asked.

"No. But she kind of looks like the one that was hanging around the barn while we were getting ready to decorate. I saw it several times, but I never stopped work to pet it. I do believe the other girls did though."

"I see."

"Sometimes barn cats can be pretty wild, but this one seems like a pet that maybe got pregnant and someone didn't want to deal with it. That happens a lot when you have a farm. People drop off their unwanted animals like somehow you're better suited to take care of them than they are."

He didn't say anything, but that seemed counterintuitive. From what he understood, farmers often had less money than regular people. Sure, they had the ground, but a cat still needed shots and to be fixed, and that cost money.

He shoved those thoughts aside without resolving them as she put two more fingers out and stroked down the head of the cat.

"She's letting me touch her okay. I... I'm not sure that it's going to hurt the kitten if I grab a hold of it, but it might already be dead."

"I know nothing about this." He felt compelled to tell her that, even though she probably already knew it. It wasn't that he knew Eleanor that well. He really didn't. But he knew of her, and he assumed she recognized him since she had come over to ask him to dance.

That was an awkwardness that he didn't want to have to deal with, but they probably would need to face it before the night was through.

But not now.

The cat gave a keening cry again and shifted, dumping off the first kitten that had been nosing around trying to find a place to nurse.

"I want to help her, but the idea of grabbing a hold of the kitten and pulling is...not a good one," he mumbled.

"That's not my favorite idea either, but I don't know of any others. I think from kind of watching, that as she pushes, I haven't seen the kitten move out at all. It makes me feel like that's our only choice."

"Do you want me to do it?"

"I guess I would prefer that, but I think I'd better. I probably have a little bit more experience with animals than you do. Unless you have experience that I don't know about?" She looked at him, and even though it was dark behind the glare of the phone flashlight, he could see the hopeful look in her eyes.

"No. I have no experience."

"That's what I thought." She let out a sigh, and then she said, "I'm going to turn the flashlight off for a minute. Just as the door opened, my sister texted me and wanted to make sure that I was okay. I better let her know that I'm good, and then we'll get to work on this." She gave a humorless laugh. "And then we'll work on our other problems."

The way she said it sounded a little funny to him, or maybe he was just stressed and needed a relief, because she made him laugh.

She sent a quick text, then aimed the flashlight of her phone back at the kitty, who was crying again.

"It sounds terrible," he said, wishing for the millionth time that there was something he could do to fix it.

"I know. I think once we get the kitten out though, she'll be fine."

"I hope so."

She nodded, then gave him the phone. "Do you mind holding this?"

"Not at all." He felt he would rather have something to do, although he was happy that it wasn't anything that was a life-or-death thing.

"All right. The next time I can see her pushing, I'm going to try to tug gently. Not hard. I don't want to pull too hard."

She was mumbling to herself, and he found himself nodding in agreement. She didn't want to pull too hard and...pull the head off? He didn't even want to go there. But he appreciated her being careful.

"All right. She's pushing." Eleanor seemed to need to talk in order to psych herself into helping or something. He wasn't sure what, but after she said that, she shifted the kitten's head first one way and then the other as though she were trying to find a good position for it to slide out.

The cat howled and stood up.

"Do you want me to hold her down?" he asked, hoping she declined his offer.

"Let's try a couple more times. She'll settle back down. I think the kitten slid just a little bit. I could be wrong, but I thought I felt it."

"All right." He tried not to sound as relieved as he felt.

He could only imagine how Eleanor must feel. But she seemed rather cool and collected. Which he had to admit was impressive. If he had to touch the kitten, he thought he might be panicking. Especially when the cat howled and jumped up.

"At least she didn't run away," Eleanor murmured as the cat settled back down, making noises in the back of her throat.

"And she's sniffing the other one. Looks like she'll take it if she can." He'd heard that animals sometimes rejected their babies. He didn't know if that was applicable to cats or not, but he supposed it could be. He wouldn't want to have anything to do with something that was causing him so much pain.

As the cat settled down, her sides heaved again. Eleanor put one hand on her head, stroking gently, and used her other hand to carefully pull the kitten, tugging it one way and then another, as though trying to slip it out by angling it a little bit. It was wise, rather than just trying to pull it straight out, and he thought it worked, even though the cat's howls made it sound like she was torturing her.

The cat jumped up and walked around again, her tail swishing in jerky motions, the kitten hanging half out.

"I think we'll have it with another push," Eleanor said, and she sounded worried and anxious.

"It's definitely out a little more than what it was."

"It's so big."

They were both quiet while the cat, still making noises, settled back down, although she was obviously in distress and anxious.

Eleanor put her hand back on the cat's head, stroking gently, which seemed to calm her a bit.

Not that Franklin was any great judge of cats and their emotions.

The cat's sides lifted up, and Eleanor didn't say anything this time, stroking the cat with one hand and doing her gentle angling tugs with the other.

The cat howled and stood, and the kitten slipped out.

It didn't move.

Franklin's heart was in his throat as he watched carefully, hoping that it just needed a moment to lie there and recover, and it would gasp for breath and start to meow. Or make the little mewing sounds the other kitten was making.

It felt like forever. Eleanor's finger touched it, stroking gently, massaging its side. It shuddered, then its mouth opened and closed and its side went up and down.

He let out the breath he hadn't been aware he had been holding.

They both sat there in silence as the cat moved around to lick the kitten, and they couldn't see it any longer.

Franklin was thrilled Eleanor had been able to get it out. Thrilled that the cat seemed like she was going to be okay.

"You did a good job," he said, keeping his voice low but unable to keep from allowing his relief and excitement from coloring it.

"I'm just glad we were here. If we hadn't been, the cat probably would have died. I don't think she was going to have that on her own."

He had to agree. "I guess, I wasn't exactly angry with being practically kidnapped or at least deceived, but you're right. If the cat had been at the dance, most likely no one would have heard her."

"Or she might have found a quieter place to have her kittens. She might have ended up outside, where no one was around to bother her, and no one could hear her, either. I... I guess everything happens for a reason, and we can find that reason if we're not so blinded by..."

"Anger? Irritation?" he asked as he handed her phone back.

"I was thinking embarrassment, but that was my feeling, not yours. After all, you don't know this, but Sally talked to me about what she was going to do, and while I told her I thought it was a silly idea, I apparently was unsuccessful in talking her out of it. I can't believe an adult person would think kidnapping a grown man was okay."

"But we just agreed that it was all for the best. The cat's alive, and both kittens will probably survive, because of Sally's harebrained scheme."

Eleanor shook her head, and then she said, "I can't believe you're not angry. I know I would be if I were you."

"Even if it saved the cat?"

"Well, I don't know about that, but I suppose you're right. Saving the cat and kittens was a nice perk. And I guess it's worth it to be stuck here in the snowstorm. Because I'm not sure we're going to get back. It was snowing pretty good when I walked in, and I can't imagine it got any better."

As she said that, her phone flashlight blinked off.

"You turned that off yourself, right?" Franklin said without moving. He didn't like being here in the dark. He had managed to sit, waiting for someone to come, because he convinced himself it wasn't going to be long. But what Eleanor had just said about them possibly being there for the length of the storm, and with her phone shutting off immediately, he had to admit something slippery, and not very happy, slid down his backbone.

"It was at seven percent. I'm pretty sure that was my phone saying goodbye."

"Great." There was a heavy dose of sarcasm in his voice. But he couldn't help it. He wasn't upset earlier because he thought he'd be rescued, but now... And they were going to be stuck in the dark.

And then he thought about the cold. They could freeze to death. He couldn't let that happen. If nothing else, he would have to make sure that Eleanor stayed warm. Some kind of protective instinct rose up in him. Maybe it was the male gene, knowing that he was supposed to be the protector, but whatever it was, he knew he would sacrifice in order to make sure Eleanor was okay.

He supposed, at some point, he would think back and be appreciative for that moment. Because up until that point in his life, he didn't know for sure whether he would have the maturity, or the character, to want to take care of someone else over himself. If nothing else, this experience, which was far from over, had taught him that much about himself.

Chapter 7

Eleanor sat in front of the cat in the dark, relief that she was able to get the kitten out, and at least save the life of the cat, and possibly the life of the kitten that had already been born, making her weak.

Knowing that the large kitten had made it, and that was almost certainly because of Sally's scheme, made her unable to be angry.

But she supposed there really wasn't any time to be angry anyway. Considering that her phone had just clicked off, Franklin didn't have his, and they were stuck in the cabin together. For at least the night.

"You drove here, didn't you?" Franklin said.

"I did. It was snowing pretty hard." She paused for a moment. "And I'm almost out of gas."

"Do you think you have enough to get back to Strawberry Sands at least?"

She hated the hope that was in his voice. Hated to have to crush the hope. "I might. But if I don't... Do we really want to be stuck in the car in the storm? Or would it be better to be here?"

"If we're close enough, we could walk. It must only be ten miles or so."

"That's probably right, but...neither one of us are really dressed to be out tramping for miles in the snow."

There was the off chance that something or someone would come along the road and pick them up. Of course, there was also the off chance that a snowplow wouldn't see them and would run over them.

Somehow, going to the worst-case scenario did not make her feel better.

"Maybe it's best for us to just plan on staying here tonight?" Franklin wasn't bossing her around; he had gone through all of the options that he could see and had chosen the best one. Now he was leaving it up to her.

"I think that might be right." Then she realized that he might not know everything she knew. "Sally told me that there was wood for the fire and that she left a care package for... She thought she was getting Peter, your brother."

"I figured that out before she left. I think her realizing that I was the wrong guy was the thing that scared her and made her run away."

"Yeah. She... She was afraid you were going to be angry. It was probably a fear that is justified. Because you certainly were within your rights to be upset."

"Yeah."

He didn't say anything else, and Eleanor cringed. Maybe he still was upset. He said that they both agreed that good things happened because they were here, but that didn't change the fact that he absolutely was not planning on spending the night in anything but comfortable, soft, and cozy warmth.

"Sally said there are supposed to be blankets and maybe a few other things. I'm not sure what she did with it."

Maybe she shouldn't have mentioned it until she found it. Maybe Sally had been so upset that she hadn't thought to bring it in.

She hoped not. She didn't really mind staying in the shed, but she didn't particularly want to be cold. And the only way to get warm would be to...snuggle with Franklin? He didn't seem like a very snuggly type of guy.

"That would be really nice. Do you have any idea where she put it?"

There was relief in his voice, and she was happy to be able to ease his mind a little. He was probably more upset than she was, because even though he'd grown up in Strawberry Sands, which was definitely a small town, he'd spent a lot of time in Chicago. Even his early years in Strawberry Sands would not have prepared him for roughing it in the middle of a Michigan snowstorm.

Not that she exactly had that kind of experience either, but she was definitely not as used to being pampered as he probably was.

"Let's hope there are candles or something in it," she murmured as she straightened to her feet, hearing the contented sounds of the mama cat purring as she licked and cared for her babies.

Eleanor couldn't see her at all, but hopefully she was snuggled down with them, and they would stay nice and toasty warm.

She'd seen plenty of kittens born outside and thrive, and she actually thought it was probably better for kittens to be born in the winter rather than the summer. There were a lot more predators out, plus the heat had a tendency to help diseases thrive.

"She wasn't in this room at all, was she?" she asked, knowing that there weren't very many places to search, but if they could narrow it down, that would make it easier.

"I think she led me in here." Franklin's voice sounded thoughtful. "It won't take long to look. I assume it's a bag or a box or something?"

"I'm not sure," she said. As they moved through the room, the thought came to her that Franklin, with his easygoing, laid-back personality, would be a great man to be with. If something like this didn't upset him, didn't turn him into a raving lunatic, then she couldn't think of too many situations that he wouldn't have a cool head in.

They finished searching the room and turned up nothing.

"Let's hope she dropped it out here." Eleanor put her hand on the door and pushed.

It stuck.

"Oh no," she said, panicking a little and shoving on the door.

It did not budge.

"'Oh no,' as in this is very bad, or 'oh no' as in something really terrible has happened like the door is stuck again, only both of us are on this side of it and no one's on the other side to lift up the latch and help get it unstuck?"

"The second," Eleanor said, using her fingers to try to find the little depression in the door that she had described to Franklin. "Hopefully when we got it unstuck earlier, it was all you, not me."

He laughed. "I'll take credit for that, but I'm right with you there."

She chuckled, even as her heart beat fast. It was one thing to be stuck in the shed for the duration of the snowstorm, but it was a completely different thing to be actually stuck, as in they couldn't get out. Especially considering that it was dark, cold, and her last text to her sister had been telling her that she was fine and not to worry about her, even if she couldn't get through since her cell phone was almost out of battery.

"I found a place to get my fingers in. Are you ready?" he asked after a few seconds.

"Yeah. I have mine in the depression below the latch."

"All right. On the count of three. One, two, three!"

At first, she didn't think they were going to get it, because nothing happened when she lifted up, then as they lifted and pushed, the door broke open, and they both stumbled forward.

He ran into her, then reached out to grab her to keep her from falling. Which she appreciated, since her finger was still in the depression.

"My finger's stuck," she said, explaining why she hadn't moved out of his way.

"Oh no. Did it twist?" he asked as his hands came down and one landed on her arm. It slid down to her finger, where it stuck in the door depression.

"No. It's just—" She moved a little, shifting toward him, to get her arm in the right position so she could twist her finger out.

He moved as she bumped into him, and her finger came free.

"Sorry about that."

"It's perfectly okay. I'm just glad you got it out. Does it hurt?"

"Not really. Just a little ache. It didn't break or anything, if that's what you're worried about."

"I was thinking earlier tonight that my night couldn't get any worse. That was after my brother spilt his drink on me and I got a phone call with some bad news. But then I got kidnapped, and worse than being stuck in this shed during a snowstorm would be if you had a broken finger the whole time."

"Yeah. That would be pretty awful, because I'm betting that the care package Sally left, if we can find it, doesn't have pain pills in it. That's not exactly something that screams romance."

"I'm betting you're right." Although, he didn't sound as sure as she did. Maybe because he didn't know exactly what would be in a romantic care package to begin with.

He shifted and brushed against her. "Sorry."

"You know, that's probably going to happen a good bit, especially if there aren't any candles and we end up in the dark. Just assume that if you run into me, it's okay. I'm not expecting you to be able to see me in the dark."

He laughed a little. "Thanks for being so understanding. Same for you."

"Now, if you step on my toes, that's a completely different story."

He laughed again. "My toes stick out further than yours do, so you might want to be careful with what you're saying there."

"Are you saying I'm clumsy or that you are?"

"Nope. Just saying you're more likely to step on my toes, since they stick out. I wasn't saying anything about you being clumsy. Although you are the one who got your finger stuck in the door."

"You're rubbing that in? You barely even know me, and you declined my invitation to dance earlier, so you probably should be nice and soothe my hurt feelings."

She couldn't believe she brought that up. She wanted to brush it under the rug. But there was a part of her that understood that they were going to be spending the night together and probably the day tomorrow. Unless some brave soul came out to rescue them. Regardless, she was going to be spending a lot of time with him, and she didn't want that hanging over her head the whole time, where she was trying to duck away from it. She figured the best thing she could do was to face it head-on.

"What was wrong with you?" He laughed. "Sorry. That wasn't a very well-formed question. Let me see if I can phrase that a little bit differently."

"It's okay. I was talking gibberish. And I don't know exactly why. Have you ever just had your tongue and your brain not work in sync? Like usually it's just a word that you mess up where you're trying to say today and tomorrow and you end up saying taymorday or something like that, but you know what I mean?"

That didn't exactly explain everything that was going on. It was a start.

"Kinda?"

"I was nervous. And that made it worse." She was glad it was dark and he couldn't see her face. Glad they were having this discussion where she could hide under the cloak of invisibility.

"I guess. I suppose I've never had trouble quite that bad though. And when you explain it like that, I understand what you're saying, but to see you in front of me not making any sense, I wasn't sure whether you were just being a goof-off, or if you had a serious problem."

"I guess you could have thought I had a stroke."

"Something like that. Although that didn't occur to me."

"I escaped from the insane asylum?"

"I thought I knew who you were, so I thought that and I hadn't heard you'd been arrested or taken into custody for anything, or that probably would have been my first thought."

"Nice. I'm super happy that I made a great impression on you." She rolled her eyes. She couldn't have been any more embarrassed.

"Well, I can't really argue with that, because yeah. You were more scary than attractive, but your second impression was pretty darn good."

"Where I opened the door and got you out of the room?"

"Kind of forgot about that. Unbelievably. I was thinking about you delivering the kitten."

"That made a good impression?"

"You saved the kitten and probably the cat as well."

"Hopefully. I don't know if helping to deliver it will cause any problems or not. But I'm hoping not."

As they talked, they'd been moving around the room. Without saying anything, she'd started moving in one direction and he'd started moving in the other.

"Hey. I just felt something."

She heard rustling as he must have bent down to check.

"It's a stove."

"Yeah. I forgot it had a small woodstove."

"I heard we had wood outside in the back, so... If we can just find some matches or something, we'll have heat."

She was hopeful. Even if they didn't have matches, what else did they have to do all night other than rub two sticks of wood together, right? Was it actually possible to start a fire like that? She wasn't sure. She'd never done it.

For now, she was going to hold onto the hope that they would find a care package and it would include matches.

Her foot touched something, and her heart stuttered.

She stopped carefully and bent down in the dark, slowly so she didn't bump into anything.

"I think I found something."

It was just to the right of the door, like Sally might have thrown it in quickly. It didn't feel huge, and it wasn't particularly heavy. As her fingers moved around it, it felt like a duffel.

"I feel a zipper. This is like a backpack or a duffel bag or something."

"Awesome. I'll keep looking. Maybe she had two."

She smiled but didn't allow the laugh that tickled the back of her throat to come out. She thought it was funny that he thought the more the better.

She appreciated his optimism though and hoped he was right.

She knelt down beside the duffel, finding the end of the zipper and grabbing it in her fingers.

The sound of the zipper opening was loud in the silence of the shed. Using her fingers made her realize how cold they were.

Lord, some matches would be really, really nice.

He knew what they needed, and if they were supposed to spend the night without fire, God knew.

Her fingers touched something cool and hard and round. A candle? If there was a candle, there was almost certainly matches.

"I think there's a candle," she said as she became more sure. The top had a stopper in it, and she used both hands to pull it out, then she loosened the lid and pulled it off.

"Yes. It's a candle!" It smelled like cinnamon, or maybe cinnamon mixed with vanilla perhaps. A Christmas candle.

"Where there's a candle, there's probably matches," Franklin said, his voice holding as much excitement as she'd heard since she'd walked into the shed.

"Exactly my thoughts," she said, setting the candle on the floor and putting her hands back in the bag. "I feel blankets and some packages... I think I might feel bread. We'll have sandwiches!"

"Awesome. I guess all of the excitement has worked up an appetite, because I'm starved."

"I was thinking I should have eaten more at the dance, but I was so busy trying to get everything organized to make sure things ran okay, I didn't even think about it."

"Yeah, I was a little preoccupied."

He had mentioned before that he had gotten a phone call with bad news. She wondered if that was what he was referring to now.

They would have time to talk about it, most likely.

"Do you think there's any chance of anyone coming out for us?"

"Maybe. I could see my brothers doing it, although with the snow, I could also see them taking people home from the barn dance who had gotten stranded or didn't want to drive in the storm."

"And they'd just forget about you?"

"Well, I had told my sister I was okay. That's the last text she got from me, and I also said that my phone was almost out of battery, so if she didn't hear from me, she would know not to worry." Her fingers touched a rectangular object. "And I hate to say this, but it's possible that they'll think it's a good idea for us to be stuck together."

Her fingers closed around the object, and she pulled it out. "I'm pretty sure these are matches."

She didn't give him a chance to answer anything about what she had said. She was going to be mortified if she had to explain to him that her family, particularly her friends, might think it was a good idea for her to be trapped with some man for an entire night and possibly a day, because that just sounded like she was desperate to get married and would do anything to have that happen. Even though he would know that it had nothing to do with her. That she hadn't instigated it in any way.

Regardless, it wasn't the thing that she really wanted to lead with.

It wasn't something she wanted to say at all.

Plus, he'd heard her ask him to dance. He would think that he would know exactly why she wasn't married. If she couldn't get her words out but sounded like someone who was either drunk or had some major problems, he wouldn't be questioning why she wasn't married. And he would probably think he totally understood why she needed to be shut in with someone.

She pulled a match out of the box and struck it along the side. It flared to life. Her lips curved up in a smile as she raised her eyes and saw Franklin grinning as well.

That look communicated a lot without words, their relief, their excitement, and their happiness.

She grabbed the candle and lit it, knowing that they probably weren't going to have to conserve matches but not wanting to waste one just in case.

"That is one of the best things I've seen all day." Franklin spoke with finality. Then he stammered a bit. "Not that the decorations at the barn dance weren't very nice."

She laughed, somehow pleased that he remembered that she'd been in charge of them. "You know, I'm with you. I thought the decorations were really nice, if I do say so myself, but the matches and the flame? Yeah. Best thing all day. All week. Possibly in my life."

They laughed together before she set the candle down, putting the match in the lid and grabbing the bag.

"There are two blankets," she said as she pulled them out. "And these are cold cuts, and there is a loaf of bread. They didn't give us any mayonnaise or mustard, but I'm just thrilled that we're not going to starve to death, and I'm not going to complain about it."

"Me either. I always wondered what was in a romantic bundle, and now I know."

She chuckled. "I thought maybe you got quiet when I said that and perhaps you were wondering what exactly that would contain."

"I've never been involved in anything that had to do with a romantic bundle. So, this has been educational in more ways than one."

Maybe he was thinking about the cat. She was.

"We could probably save some cold cuts for the cat," he said, his voice holding a bit of a question.

"Yeah. I couldn't sit here and eat without making sure that she got something as well."

"Then I guess the next thing we need to do is to start a fire?" It was another question that was said more like a statement as he moved across the room and stopped beside her.

"I think that's right. I'm pretty sure we'll have to bring wood in from outside."

He didn't say anything else but walked to the door and opened it.

Everything was white. Where there had been just a few flurries starting to come down when she arrived, the entire world was now blanketed in white, and there were at least two inches on the top of her car.

"You were right about it coming down fast," he said, his eyes widening. "I have to admit I held out some hope that we would be able to go home."

"We can still try if you want to. But my tires are bald. I've been meaning to put on the winter tires before winter, but with all the planning that I was doing with the barn dance, I just ran out of time. Plus, it was kind of expensive, so I was putting it off as long as possible." She almost didn't admit that last part, but she didn't see any reason to try to pretend that she was anything that she wasn't. Money was tight for a dog groomer, and she would be silly to pretend otherwise.

"Well, I guess I wish that had been different, but I think at this point, we're better off staying and making do with what we have. Which is food and heat, and maybe we can figure out a way to melt some snow and get some water."

"Actually, I think there are a couple bottles in the bottom. I assumed it was water, but I just didn't say." She should have gotten all the things out and lined them up.

"Anything else?" he asked, looking back toward the duffel.

"I think there might have been some chocolate in there too. At least, it felt like a box that's long and low, and I assumed it was candy. But being that getting the matches and the blankets and the food was so exciting, the candy kinda slipped my mind."

"Candy is food."

"True," she said, laughing. It was funny, she wouldn't have thought being trapped with Franklin would be fun. Maybe it wouldn't have been if he had been angry. The fact that he'd taken everything so calmly, that he hadn't gotten upset, he wasn't railing against her friends or telling her how stupid she was, or anything like that. He'd absorbed the fact that his evening wasn't going the way he planned, and he'd been a great guy to be around.

She was...actually having fun. If she were being honest with herself, she thought she might actually be disappointed if they got rescued.

Wasn't that sad? It probably said something about the state of her life, more than anything else, although it was most likely a huge compliment to Franklin as well.

Probably he was surrounded by women eager for his attention when he was in Chicago. That might have been another reason that he found her so distasteful when she stood in front of him at the barn dance. She squirmed a little at the thought.

"I'm pretty sure the wood is behind the shed. That's where it always was, and if we're lucky, it'll be nice and rotted, and there will be some kindling at the bottom of the pile."

"All right. I think we should leave the candle in here?"

"Yes, it should be light enough to see without it. I could be wrong. Sometimes when it's snowing, the cloud cover makes everything really dark, but usually the white reflects any light that's out there."

He nodded, then walked out the door. She followed, thinking that the least she could do was to try to make him as comfortable as possible, since he had responded in the very best way anyone could have to the circumstances. It made her a little sad to think he might not be enjoying himself quite as much as she was, and if there was anything she could do to make being stuck with her more fun for him, she would definitely give it a try.

Chapter 8

Franklin held the match to the small pile of rotted wood and hoped it would catch quickly and easily. He knew that was probably a little far-fetched, but it would be really nice to have a fire. He wasn't cold exactly, but once they had a fire, he felt like he could relax. They wouldn't freeze to death, and they definitely weren't going to starve overnight. There had been water at the bottom of the bag along with candy, just as Eleanor said, and they were pretty much set. As long as they had a fire.

Eleanor had gone back out for another armful of wood, and it was a little surprising to him, since they hadn't been together very long, but he missed her presence. She didn't have to be talking to just make him feel less alone.

Maybe that was just because they were out in the middle of nowhere and it was dark and cold, so it was nice to have another human around.

He could say that to himself, but he knew it was a little bit more than that.

He didn't know too many other women who would have been able to do what Eleanor had. Not just in delivering the kitten, but in staying calm and not panicking. She wasn't hanging onto him, begging him to save her, but she wasn't being bossy and acting like she knew it all either. Most of all, she wasn't having hysterics, but had a cool head, and was helping with their survival, if he could use that term, although it made it seem like they were on the verge of dying. Perhaps they would be if they didn't have a fire.

They still might, he thought to himself, as the flame didn't catch.

"I was hoping it would just catch, and a big fire would start to roar, and everything would be okay," he said as she came in the door and he reached back to grab another match out of the box.

"I think it will. I really don't think it's going to be hard. But I could be wrong."

She'd been right about most things, and he had a good mind to trust her. She knew a lot more about this kind of stuff than he did, but she wasn't acting like it. Which he appreciated.

It turned out, she was right about the fire catching. It took three matches, but on the third match, the wood started to flame, and it continued to flame after the match went out.

Carefully he blew on it, then added a few more small pieces, and soon he had a small but cheerful fire.

"Well, that's very Christmasy," Eleanor said as she watched the flames dance in the doorway of the stove.

He laughed. "I wasn't thinking Christmasy, but I suppose that's an adjective that would suit."

"What were you thinking? Warm? Lifesaving?"

"Yeah. Pretty much a lifesaver. I don't think we would have frozen to death, but I'm pretty sure we would have gotten to know each other a lot better than what we do now."

She laughed, like the idea didn't bother her at all. He kind of thought it didn't. Although she'd been careful, after they'd run into each other opening the door, not to touch him.

After all, they were practically strangers.

"I guess we really don't have water to wash our hands, but I wouldn't mind a sandwich."

They might as well eat, then see if they couldn't get some rest.

"I washed mine off a little bit in the snow. My fingers were already freezing, and I figured it wouldn't hurt to get a little bit colder. Especially after I touched the kitten."

"Do... Do you want to check on her?" They hadn't done that yet, but in the back of his mind, he wanted to see. Wanted to be sure that the kittens and the cat were all okay.

"Yeah. Good idea," she said, grabbing the candle and standing up.

As long as he left the door to the stove open, the room had a cheerful glow, with long, dancing shadows. He had a gas fireplace in his condo in Chicago, but it didn't quite have the personality that the wood fire did. That made sense, since it wasn't exactly a real fire.

He had often wondered why people might prefer the mess and dirt of wood to gas, but he could kind of see now why they might. The flames were cheerful in a way that gas wasn't, and it cast a glow that seemed cozy and cute and thankfully threw a lot of heat.

He followed her into the back room, afraid of what they might see. They hadn't heard anything else out of the cat, and he had been busy with the fire and hadn't thought about what that could mean.

But as soon as they stepped in, the glow from the candle showed that there was movement on the rags at least.

"She had another one!" Eleanor said right away.

He blinked, then looked again. "Two. She has four total. So she must've had two more." He counted once more just to be sure. They were all about the same size, except for the one they pulled, which was obviously bigger, and they were all nose to their mom's belly, nursing.

They didn't say anything more, but just stood and watched the newborns nurse for a bit. He couldn't help smiling as he watched. They were so sweet and cute, and such a contrast to the raging storm and harsh weather outside. He wanted to say something to that effect but couldn't think of how to phrase it so it didn't sound sappy, and he quit thinking about it when his stomach growled loudly and broke the silence in the room.

"Sounds like it's time to eat," Eleanor said with a smile as she turned and walked out of the small room.

"Sorry about that," he mumbled. He couldn't remember the last time he'd been that hungry, and the noises his stomach made were embarrassing.

"I'm glad, because I'm hungry. But I didn't want to eat if you weren't ready."

"That was considerate of you."

"I try," she said, with a little bit of humor in her voice which he enjoyed. She wasn't afraid to make fun of herself. Some people took themselves too seriously, and he appreciated a person who could laugh and make fun of themselves and just enjoy life.

He supposed he had a tendency to be too serious, and part of the reason he'd agreed to work with Noah at building the hotel and possibly moving to Strawberry Sands was so that he could slow down and enjoy life a little more.

They ate their sandwiches in silence, sitting on the floor in front of the stove.

He had his about half gone when Eleanor said, "So, I've been trying to figure out whether it's better for both of us to get a blanket, and we each have our own blanket, or whether we should share? Please don't take it wrong, I... I just figured I'd throw it out there so I can stop worrying about it."

"If you're worried, we'll just do whatever makes you feel okay."

"Well, not worried about it exactly, I just... It's just kind of an awkward thing that I didn't want to suggest we share, but if I'm being honest, the fire is nice but I'm freezing."

"All right. We'll share. And being that the stove is so small, I don't think we're going to be able to get a fire that's much bigger. And there is no insulation at all to help keep the heat in."

"I agree. I'm just happy that there actually was a woodstove in here. I suppose, if it happens again, we could request a bigger stove."

"This is not going to happen again." He said that firmly but with a smile. Seriously. How many people in their entire lives got stuck in a shack in a snowstorm? "You know we belong to a very elite group."

"Huh?" she asked, not following him at all.

"How many people have gotten stuck in a shack in a snowstorm? We have to be one of what? Hundreds? Thousands? If there are eight billion people in the world, that puts us in a small group."

"Well, I think probably the thing that sets us apart is the fact that I have friends who would actually think that this was a good idea. A good...trick, for lack of a better word, to play on someone."

"That's true. I don't have any friends like that. I just happened to get drawn into this, I want to say because of you, but it's really because of Peter. I suppose we can just blame everything on Peter."

"He sounds like a great person to take all the blame. A fun guy."

That's what everyone thought. Franklin was the stick-in-the-mud, and Peter was the fun one. Figures that Eleanor would feel the same way.

"Did you think I was Peter when you asked me to dance?" He didn't really mean to ask that question, but it came out anyway.

Her eyes grew big, and she glanced at him. "No! Not at all. I knew who you were." Her brows drew down. "Why? Did you think that because Sally got confused?"

"I guess."

"Well, you were wearing his cowboy hat when she saw you, right?"

He nodded. After he made the fire, he'd taken it off and set it down on top of the duffel bag. "I also have his shirt on. After he spilled his punch on mine, he gave me his, because he had an extra one out in his truck."

"I can see how she'd get confused. Your hair is the same color, and with that hat on, you guys have the same chin shape."

He understood what she was saying and agreed. "I didn't know that taking my brother's shirt was going to cause such a problem." He almost said that if he had to do it over again, he would refuse the shirt and wear the dirty one. But... While he had been annoyed at first, especially after Sally closed the door and ran away and he was alone, he...couldn't be upset about the way the evening had turned out.

Maybe, maybe if the storm was really bad and they ended up stuck and freezing to death, he would be more upset, but he couldn't believe how chill he was about it.

Part of him whispered in his ear that it was because of Eleanor. He hadn't been impressed with her when she had asked him to dance, apparently, but there had been something kind of enjoyable about the evening.

"You know, I don't have too many opportunities to do life-and-death situations in my life. If this situation can even be called this."

"It could be. If we hadn't had a fire, I think I would have suggested that we try to get back to town. It's going to get really cold overnight as the storm moves through, and hypothermia and freezing to death is nothing to mess with."

"I guess I just... I'm not as upset as what I would have thought I would have been. And it's surprising me."

"I suppose I'm with you a little bit. I wasn't locked in, and I had a choice about coming, so I'm not trying to compare our situations. But I was pretty upset at Sally for doing something so dumb. But I have to admit, I've kind of been having a good time."

He smiled at those words. She was basically saying the same thing he was, and it was hard to believe. He would never have thought in a million years that he would actually enjoy something like this. He should be angry, demanding to go home, complaining about Sally, and longing for a do-over where he could keep his own shirt on, but he almost felt like maybe he should go home and thank Peter for spilling that punch. If he hadn't, he wouldn't have been here.

But there was the small matter of how they were going to spend the night. He watched as she grabbed the blankets out of the bag and shook them out.

"This one is slightly bigger. Let's give that to you." She held up the darker of the two blankets. He thought the color was blue, but with the orange flames, he couldn't be sure.

"I'll take the smaller one."

"No. It makes more sense for me to take it, since I'm smaller."

He took the blanket she handed him without further comment. He didn't want to make suggestions on how they should sleep, since he didn't want to make her uncomfortable. Maybe if they were both curled up under their blanket next to the stove, they would be okay.

"This is a little awkward," she said as she bit her lip.

"Same," he said, relieved that she was going to admit it and maybe they were going to talk about it, instead of just ignoring the fact that somehow they were going to have to figure out a way to sleep with a total stranger tonight.

Only she really wasn't a total stranger. They'd known each other a little since he'd started building the hotel, and after the last few hours, they definitely were no longer strangers.

"So, I guess I'll just say, I think probably the best idea is for us to lie down side by side and share both blankets. I'm not trying to hit on you or anything like that—"

"I didn't think you were. And that was what I was thinking too, but I didn't want to suggest it, because I didn't want to come off like that either."

She gave him a relieved look. "I think we'll be okay. Truly, but I do think it's smart to share the warmth that we have. This shed is not insulated at all, and the heat from the fire is going to blow out."

"I'm assuming we'll probably have to get up and throw wood on the fire several times as well."

"I agree. And maybe we should bring in a few more armloads of wood, so no one has to go outside in the middle of the night." She bit her lip and looked at the flue pipe where it came up from the stove and then went into the wall.

"What's the matter?" He didn't like the look on her face.

"I don't really have any experience in flues or fires. We've always had some other kind of heat source. But... I think I remember hearing about people cleaning their flues, and I was just trying to remember what makes the flue catch on fire."

"If this catches on fire, it's going to go pretty fast."

"It is, and... I just... I was just a little worried about it, that's all."

"We could take turns staying up."

"I don't feel like I'm going to sleep at all. I'm tired but I'm wired if that makes sense."

"Typically when I lie down, I can sleep pretty much anywhere, so while I would say that I'm not tired, I know once my head hits the pillow," he laughed a little, "the floor in this case, I think I'll be out pretty fast."

She nodded, looking at the floor and then looking back at the stovepipe. "Do you think we should move the kittens into the room with us? Just in case we have to leave fast?"

"That's a good idea. I wouldn't want you to get stuck in a burning building just because you didn't want to leave the kittens." He paused for a moment, liking the fact that she thought about the animals and her concern wasn't just for herself. He'd been noticing that, that she thought about him as much as she thought about herself.

"How about you move the kittens, and I'll get a couple more armloads of wood." He took a breath. "You don't think moving them will make the mother not take them or anything, do you?" He wished he had more experience in that. Or even more, he wished he had his phone so he could Google it. But they were just going to have to go with what they knew, which was a little different than normal, since they could typically look anything up on their phones at any time. It was a little hard to get used to not being able to.

"I don't know. But I do know that it will be safer for her to be in the room with us just in case anything happens."

"It's not like she can go anywhere anyway."

"Exactly."

They didn't say anything more while he went one way out the door, and she went the opposite direction to get the cat.

He brought four more loads of wood in and stacked them neatly beside the stove while she arranged the cat and her kittens in a snug little nest on the opposite wall.

She hadn't wanted them to get too hot, and he had to agree with that as well. Every time he brought an armload of wood in, she left what she was doing and helped stack it, so they were both done at pretty much the same time.

"I'm gonna run out and wash my hands in the snow," he said as he brought the fourth load in.

She nodded. "I'll go with you."

He held the door while she went out and marveled again at how different this was from his regular life, but how much he was… He hated to use the word enjoying it, but he kind of did.

They walked back in, with Eleanor carrying a handful of snow.

"What's up with that?" he asked, wondering if they had run out of water.

"I thought I would melt it for the cat. I had broken up a little bit of my sandwich and saved it, and I have that along with a jar lid that I was going to put the snow in for her. She wasn't really interested in it the last time I offered it."

"Maybe because she just gave birth."

"Possibly."

She arranged the things for the cat while he went over and stood beside the fire, looking at the flue and wishing he had an idea of how to tell if it was going to catch on fire or not. He hadn't thought about it at all until Eleanor had said something. And then, after she'd mentioned it, he remembered that occasionally, especially in his younger years when he still read the newspaper, he'd read articles about people's houses catching on fire, starting with a fire in their flue.

He usually did fall asleep fairly quickly, but he felt like it was his job to protect. Funny how a situation like this brought that out more than anything else ever had in his life before.

Or maybe it was something else. It could be that it was because of Eleanor, coming to get him, making sure he was okay, and with every interaction she had with him, doing what she could to help and think of him.

Maybe her actions brought out the best in him.

Whatever it was, he doubted he was going to get much sleep that night.

Chapter 9

"So the duffel isn't very soft, but I guess we can use it as a pillow. And we have two more bottles of water." Eleanor bit her lip again. She'd been doing it so much that evening that it was actually sore.

She let go of it, knowing she didn't have any chapstick or anything to put on to make it feel better.

But it was a little disconcerting. Not being stuck with Franklin. That had turned out to be...not as bad as what she would have thought; even the awkwardness when they talked about her incoherent invitation to dance hadn't been that bad. But this...this trying to agree to sleep together despite the fact that she really didn't know him, and would never dream of doing this in her normal life, had made things the most awkward yet.

Still, she couldn't fault Franklin. He had been as good as a person could be under the circumstances and far better than she would have expected.

Without saying anything, he walked over and got the duffel. He set the bread out, along with the meat, which they kept in the far corner, on top of an old stand which was the only piece of furniture in the place and looked like it might collapse at any time, but so far, it kept the food off the floor.

Zipping the duffel back up, he set it at the head of the blankets.

"All right. It's after midnight, although I honestly don't feel the slightest bit tired." She didn't want to be the first person to lie down. But she knew she needed to. It was time. What else were they going to do?

She should have known that Franklin would make it so it wasn't awkward.

He lifted up the blankets that she set on the floor. "You lie down with your head on the duffel, I'll lie down behind you, and we'll arrange the blankets over the top. I'll try to get out without waking you up when I load up the fire."

"I can take a turn doing that," she volunteered immediately. She didn't want him to have to be the one to get up every time all night. Plus, she was going to be keeping an eye on it anyway. There was no way she would sleep soundly with the thought of a flue fire in her head. She had no idea when the last time anyone had used it was, and they didn't exactly have the tools or equipment or knowledge to clean it out.

"All right. Then we'll just assume that we'll add wood to the fire every hour or so. I think I've added it twice. It's small and doesn't last long."

"That sounds good to me. You've been putting about three pieces on. That's all that will fit." That sounded reasonable, and she liked that he wasn't trying to split hairs. They were just going with whatever was working.

"All right, you'll get up the next time, and I'll get up after that. I'm guessing that neither one of us are going to sleep very well."

"I think you're probably right," she said as he picked up the blankets and she knelt down, lying on her side facing the fire with her head on the duffel.

She felt him lie down beside her, and the blankets settled down over top of them. She adjusted it in front and then said, "Do you have enough to cover your back? That would probably be the most important thing, since it's the furthest from the fire."

"It's good."

He didn't say anything more, and she didn't for a while either.

They lay in silence as she watched the flames crackle and pop and the logs slowly be consumed. She'd always loved watching fire. It was kind of like watching water in a stream or river. Just always something different to see, and a nice, easy, relaxing thing to watch. Where she could let her mind wander, just think about the fire, and allow whatever came into her head to linger as long as it wanted to before it floated away.

After a while, he shifted behind her, and she realized his breathing had never settled down into the deep breathing that she would have expected from someone who was asleep.

Quietly she said, "Uncomfortable?"

He breathed out a puff of air. "Yeah. It's the floor and a duffel. I wasn't expecting to be comfortable."

"You just said that you fall asleep really easily. So, I kind of thought that you would have been asleep a long time ago."

"I usually would have been. But what you said about the flue made me realize that I probably should be keeping watch. Still, I'm not deliberately trying to stay awake."

"Me either. Maybe I'm just too keyed up to sleep, or maybe it's the hard floor. Whatever it is, I've been lying here daydreaming but not the slightest bit sleepy."

"Same. You're not scared, are you?" he asked, his voice quiet but low and rumbly and with vibrations that were not unpleasant against her back.

"No. I guess I could be, but rather than focusing on the what ifs, I try to focus on the what I can do right now to fix things."

"That's smart."

"It helps me keep my mind running over the things that I can do to help, rather than getting myself worked up and afraid of the things that might or might not happen."

"That's a good way to look at things. A great way to shape your brain."

"It didn't used to be like that," she said softly.

He paused for a moment, as though that surprised him, and then he said, "No?"

It was a question, an invitation to say more if she wanted to. Normally she would let that drop, if she had even said that much. But considering their close proximity and the fact that they were going to be spending the night together, and neither one of them would probably be sleeping much, or maybe it was just late and she was tired and didn't have as much self-control.

Or maybe she trusted him.

Whatever it was, she found herself talking about something she normally didn't.

"I struggled with anxiety, pretty bad anxiety actually. It started when I was in high school."

"High school can be pretty harsh. There are a lot of expectations and a lot of pressure. Sometimes it's really hard to handle everything that gets thrown at us. The pressure for grades and to perform and to get into the right college and to do well in every subject. Even subjects we're not good at."

"Yeah. I guess. Maybe it was that my dad left too, and Mom was alone. No one else seemed to really notice, but I was kind of sensitive to it."

"I remember that, vaguely," he murmured.

He had been there, grown up in Strawberry Sands. And they went to school together, although not in the same grade. Still, the town was small enough that everyone knew everyone else, and he would have known about her dad leaving.

"Mom did such a good job of holding everything together, but... I guess I just worried. I don't know. But I know that I had all the things that could go wrong running around my head. That's probably what the problem was."

"It's never helpful when we worry."

"No."

"I thought I remembered you having a boyfriend. So you eventually just got over it?"

She didn't know whether he was asking to make conversation, or if he was really truly interested.

"I did. I hid behind him, to some extent, I guess. The anxiety became overwhelming when I didn't have him to use as a crutch. I got to the point where I didn't even want to leave the house. He was content to come over and watch TV, and we didn't usually go anywhere. Looking back, it wasn't a great relationship, but I held onto it...I guess because of Mom and my extreme fear of...I don't even know what I was afraid of. I managed to finish school, and I was accepted at several different colleges, but I was too scared to go."

"Ouch."

"I know. That's sad, isn't it? But seriously, I just hated the idea of leaving home. And I have to admit that Mom could use the help at the bed-and-breakfast. And I took classes for my freshman and sophomore years. So it wasn't like I was sitting at home with the covers over my head. But I didn't interact with any of the guests, and I did the cleaning and cooking without talking to anyone as much as I could. And when I actually had to show up on campus for my junior year..."

"You were basically a recluse."

"Yeah. But I was so afraid that business would die down, that we would stop getting customers, that I wouldn't be able to make a living, that I actually got a dog grooming certificate online."

"Just a backup for your backup?"

"Yeah. I wasn't really expecting to use it, but once I got it, my siblings knew that I had it, and they would ask me to do their dogs or their friends' dogs. Eventually, I bought a small studio outside of town. It wasn't originally a dog groomer place, but it worked for me. I was able to get the equipment I needed inexpensively. It was the right price, and I didn't feel like I had to make a whole lot of money in order to pay my bills. I had saved enough to be able to purchase the building for cash."

"Wow."

"Yeah. Looking back, maybe that was the best thing. If I had gone to college, I definitely wouldn't have been saving my money, and I wouldn't have been able to do that."

"College takes money, and even though you feel like you work every waking second, you never really get ahead."

"Yeah. I've heard that."

"So then you just kind of outgrew your anxiety?"

"No. My boyfriend...cheated."

Chapter 10

There. She said it. Eleanor hadn't thought about it for a long time. He'd been cheating their entire relationship. She hadn't ever noticed, since she hardly ever went out and didn't talk to anyone she didn't have to.

"Ugh." Franklin sounded disgusted.

"Yeah." It had been painful. So hard. It had wiped her out emotionally, which wasn't hard in her already not-healthy state. "It took me a bit to get over that, and I suppose I never really trusted anyone outside of my family again."

"That's too bad. But that helped you get over your anxiety?"

"Some. I guess I got to the point where I was thinking about being scared that the bed-and-breakfast was going to fail, that something would happen to Mom, that something would happen to me and I couldn't work… You name it, I worried about it. I just slowly realized how ungodly that all was. How I wasn't really depending on God, I wasn't trusting Him to have good things happen to me. To take care of me."

"That's basically what anxiety is. Being worried. And we're commanded not to worry."

"I was worrying all the time. About everything. I got myself so afraid that sometimes just getting out of bed in the morning produced a panic attack. I thought there was something wrong with me, something physical. You know? Like I needed more of whatever hormone was a happy hormone."

"But there really isn't such a thing."

"Not really. I mean, I suppose there are chemical imbalances for some people, but biologically, our thoughts produce the chemicals that cause our moods. It wasn't that my body couldn't make the chemicals, it was that I wasn't giving my body the ability to make them, or I was telling it to make the wrong chemicals, because my thoughts were so negative."

"You didn't figure that out on your own." His voice rumbled against her back, and while he didn't have his arm around her, his close proximity was not just keeping her warm, but it was comforting.

"No. One morning, as I was lying in bed after having a panic attack, I hadn't even gotten up for the day, and I was scared to death, and I just couldn't figure out what I was scared to death about. I hadn't been able to eat, and I was getting worse because I was losing weight. I knew I had to do something, and I realized I had known for a while that it had to be me that did something. For a long time, I wanted someone else to come and just fix it for me, but that wasn't going to happen. It had to be me fixing myself."

"It's a pretty big step whenever we realize that we're in charge of our lives, under the authority of God of course, but we're the ones who have to make the decisions to do the things. Other people aren't going to do them for us."

"Exactly. I mean, sometimes people did do things for me, but I didn't want to be the person who is dependent on other people. I wanted to be the kind of person who could help people. And yet there I was, too scared to even get out of bed."

She lay there thinking about it for a minute. She couldn't believe that that had been a time in her life, although it felt like she had to keep focused on the positive, or that anxiety could come roaring back.

"So you started that day to make changes?"

"I had to research it first. I had the internet, and every spare second, I was researching how to handle anxiety without medication. I didn't want to be on pills for the rest of my life. But that was what was going to happen if I went to the doctor. They were going to give me anxiety pills and tell me that I had to take them, and then I'd heard that eventually they became ineffective and you had to up your dosage. It scared me, the idea of being addicted to pills and unable to function without them. That was probably the one time that my anxiety actually helped me." She laughed.

"You were too afraid to go on medication so you found a way to handle it without it?"

"Basically. So yeah, and then like you said, I figured out that I needed to focus on the positive. But not just that, I wanted to do it in a Christian way. In a way that acknowledged that God was in charge, which kind of makes me scared, because I want to be in charge, and I want to make things happen the way I want them to happen."

"That is not the way life works."

"Exactly, and it's kind of scary to lift my fingers up and allow God to do it. So what I had to do was I had to memorize verses that said that God was good. That He only wanted good things for me. And when bad things happened, I had to understand that they were only bad because I was looking at them like they were bad. Like when I lost a client. I might get scared that I was going to lose my business or lose a hundred more clients and that was just going to be terrible, or I could look at it in the way that losing one client could spur me to figure out things that I could do better so I could attract more clients. And it turned out to be a good thing."

"Because if you hadn't lost the first client, you wouldn't have been inspired to improve yourself?"

"Exactly. So the bad thing prompted good things. And I tried to shift my mindset where I wasn't scared if my income went down or if Mom would lose the bed-and-breakfast. I would just say, God's going to help me figure something else out. And then I would try to let it go. It wasn't easy at first."

"It's so hard to change our thoughts."

"It is. I kept a thankful journal though, and every night before I went to bed, I tried to write down at least five things that I was thankful for. I tried to make them different every day, so I wasn't just thanking God for the same things. And then I tried to look around during the day to find those different things. It really did help me go from seeing all the bad things to looking at the good."

"That's a smart thing to do. When you know you're going to have to find five new things to write down in the evening, it would prompt you to look a little closer at your life."

"And there was so much to be thankful for."

"And that helped you with your anxiety?"

"For the most part. I still don't do very good in social situations, like the barn dance. I don't mind working behind the scenes, but being at the front is not my favorite thing. But that could be more of a personality thing. I'm an introvert rather than an extrovert."

"I think it's perfectly normal for people to not want to draw a lot of attention to themselves at times. So I think you're right about that." He paused. "It must have taken a lot of nerve for you to go over and ask me to dance."

"It did." She laughed a little. It was almost to the point where it was funny now. "That was just my old anxiety kicking in probably. Making it so that the thing that I thought might happen—you would say no—happened, because I managed to totally mess everything up. It's like a self-fulfilling prophecy."

"I see. I wasn't very sympathetic."

"You didn't know. And you really did get a phone call. At least I assume you did?"

"I did." He didn't say anything more, but his tone indicated that the phone call wasn't a good thing, and she remembered that he mentioned that several times. That he had some bad news.

"So, I just told you my deep, dark secret," she teased. "Are you going to tell me your bad news?" She said it lightly, maybe to make sure that he wasn't taking her too seriously. She didn't go into the fact that she wasn't married because she'd been too anxious to even date for almost a decade.

Even now, the idea of going on a date wasn't exactly relaxing. While she didn't have the crippling anxiety that she had before, she just didn't feel like she had the skills. Or maybe, case in point would be her inability to even make a simple request like asking someone to dance.

Regardless, she tried to spin that in her head the way she always did. God knew. Maybe He was just having her wait for the perfect man. If she hadn't had her anxiety, she might have ended up with someone who wasn't as good as the man God had for her. Maybe she wouldn't have waited.

She didn't know, and she wouldn't know for sure until she got to heaven, if that was the type of thing they talked about in heaven. Regardless, the idea was to trust God and allow Him to dictate her life.

"I don't want to pry. You don't have to tell me."

"Oh, well, it's not that I don't want to tell you. And you're not prying. You just told me something that I'm guessing that a lot of people don't know. I mean, I lived in Strawberry Sands. It's a small town, and I didn't know anything about your anxiety."

"My family was really good about keeping it quiet. And just giving me the time and space I needed in order to figure out how to fix it. So yeah. Plus, after high school, you moved away and never really came back."

"After my parents inherited the property in Blueberry Beach and sold it, they split the profit between themselves and my siblings and me. We all got a nice, hefty inheritance, my parents sold their house in Blueberry Beach and moved to Florida. Apparently, they like the winters down there better."

She laughed at the humor in his voice. After all, if they were in Florida rather than in Strawberry Sands right now, he wouldn't be trapped in a shack with a winter storm blowing all around them.

"I guess tonight might be a good argument for Florida."

"No. I'm not upset about it. I mean, if they do it again, I guess I'd request an air mattress or something. Or two. More blankets."

"They probably put such a sparse amount of blankets in there just to make sure that the couple they were trying to get together actually had to do what we're doing right now—rely on each other for heat."

"That might be. Still, if they're going to get the wrong people, they need to have more preparations for the contingencies."

They laughed a little, and it seemed cheery and cozy, rather than cold and dreary. It wasn't hard to forget that she was lying on the hard floor and probably wouldn't get any sleep. Somehow it felt like...not a magical night, but a good one.

"The phone call was from a business associate. She doesn't work for my company, we knew each other from seeing each other around various business functions."

"Okay," she said as he paused.

"We met at a business function that we both attended dateless. We got to talking, and while we didn't hit it off romantically, we made an agreement that if we didn't have a date, and we needed one, we'd be each other's go-to person. She's a nice lady, and I like her okay, but...not like that."

"And she feels the same about you."

"Yeah. Exactly. It's a no-pressure situation."

"Well, that is nice. So the phone call... It was her changing her mind? Or finding someone new?"

"No. I guess that would be kind of a bummer too, but her sister has malaria and she's in some African country. Zimbabwe or something. Anyway, Maisie was telling me that she needed to go to her sister immediately, not just because she was sick, but because the hospitals aren't that great in those third world countries, and she wanted to make sure she was getting the best care possible. Of course I understood that."

"Of course. She could die."

"Exactly. So I feel a little guilty because I felt annoyed because the reason she was calling was because I have my company's annual Christmas charity event this weekend, and she was going to be my date. I'm the head of the company, and I'm going to be in the public eye a good bit. Now… I'm going to be dateless. She wasn't just a date, but she also helped me a lot. So, I lost my help and my date, and now I'm stuck here and can't really do anything to fix it."

"That's terrible." She didn't know what else to say. She didn't really know much about company charity events or big galas or anything of that nature, but she did understand the idea that it was easier to face something like that with someone reliable beside a person. Someone he could count on and depend on. Someone who would make things a little easier for him.

"It's not the end of the world. Although, I don't really have anyone else to ask. I've been thinking that I'll probably just go by myself, but it's going to be a lot harder. She really helped me with the silent auction especially. And that is our big fundraiser for the year, where we donate all the proceeds to the Chicago Midtown Humane Society."

"Sounds like something near and dear to my heart," she said, smiling a little. She donated plenty of time to the humane society in Blueberry Beach. When they had adopt-a-pet days, she would give pets baths, groom them, and even put little ribbons in their fur and make them look cute for people to adopt.

She loved taking an animal that looked a little mangy and unkempt and giving them what basically amounted to a makeover.

"I guess you're a pet groomer. It makes sense."

"Yeah. I'm pretty active with the humane society in Blueberry Beach. There isn't one here, so their jurisdiction comes up this way."

"Interesting." The fire had died down, and he stirred behind her. "I'm going to throw a few more logs on the fire."

"It's my turn." She moved, but he put a hand on her hip, and she froze.

"I'll get it. I'm awake. Just let me, okay?"

She nodded, then realized that her back was to him and he might not see her.

"All right," she said.

His hand lifted a moment later, and the heat that had been against her back disappeared. The covers fell back down as he stood, and he arranged them so that she was not uncovered, but it wasn't the same. She missed his warmth.

Not that she was cold. She'd been nice and toasty since they lay down.

He threw a couple of logs on the fire then brushed his hands off.

"Do you want anything while I'm up?" he asked.

"No thank you," she said without looking at him, her eyes on the fire. She was trying to think of someone that he could take. Someone who would be a good date for him to help him with his gala. Unfortunately, she really didn't know anyone.

He got a drink of water from the bottle that sat on the floor before he came over and slipped back under the covers.

"It gets cool pretty fast once the fire burns down," he said, resuming the place that he had right up against her back.

"I really miss your heat when you are gone, I can't imagine how it must have felt to get out of the covers."

"I guess I could add that to my list of things I think they need to fix if they do this again. They need to choose a place where there is insulation, and it doesn't get quite so cold."

"Again, I think that probably serves their purposes. If she had gotten Peter in here with Norma Jean the way she wanted to, she would want them snuggled up together."

"I wonder if they talked to Peter at all. I kind of think that he might have been concerned about finding me. At the very least, I'd expect him to be a little bit worried. I don't usually disappear without saying anything to anyone."

"I'm sure everyone knew. In fact, it would shock me if they didn't."

Chapter 11

Lena looked around with a smile at the inside of the barn. In all her years in Strawberry Sands, she'd never dreamed they'd have a dance like this. Or that her daughter Eleanor, of all people, would be the one to spearhead the majority of it.

Of course, Eleanor had had a whole army of helpers, but considering what Eleanor had gone through as a late teen and early adult, the anxiety that she struggled with, and the victory she finally had over it, Lena couldn't be happier.

"I think we have a problem, Mom," Sunday said as she stopped beside her. It was the first time that evening Lena had seen Sunday without Noah beside her. The two had been inseparable since earlier that year, and since their marriage, it was like they'd become attached or something.

Lena was so happy to see it. It thrilled her soul to see her daughters, and her sons, making smart choices about their life partners. Unlike her.

As always, a small feeling of sadness went through her at the thought of her failed marriage, her cheating husband, and the years she'd spent alone, raising her children by herself.

That hadn't been the plan. Not her plan anyway. The Lord had seen her through it all. And she couldn't fault Him at all. But still, there was a little piece of her that wished she had had that for herself. A life partner. Someone to walk through the trials and tribulations that beset humans on this planet. Someone to share her joys and her sorrows. Someone to share the workload. To share the fun times too. Someone to whisper to late at night when she woke up with something on her mind. Someone to talk to when she couldn't sleep. Someone to smile at over her morning coffee.

But that hadn't been her lot in life, and she tried to be grateful anyway. Her life had been a good one.

Not that it was over. Far from over. But Noah was buying the bed-and-breakfast, the sale would be final in March, and she would be an employee, rather than a business owner.

Their deal had been that she would get the little bungalow that Clara had spent a lot of time in before she got married.

Lena was a little bit sad at moving out of the bed-and-breakfast, and Sunday and Noah had not insisted on it at all. In fact, they wanted her to stay.

But sometimes in order to step through a new door, a person had to leave the spot they were in.

Shaking those thoughts off, Lena allowed the Christmas music and the lights and all of the beautiful decorations to soothe her soul as she looked at her beloved daughter.

"What's going on?" she asked easily, knowing that there wasn't anything serious. The night had been a resounding success.

"Well, it's kind of complicated, but apparently Sally Mintz kidnapped Franklin, Noah's business partner, and is holding him hostage on his brother's farm."

"What?" Lena said, snapping out of her dreamy reverie immediately.

"Yeah. I know, it's kind of crazy, but that's exactly what's going on. I don't know what got into Sally, other than she's been taking care of Wilma for so long, she just needed... Maybe she just needs more help than what we've been giving her."

"I see." She made a mental note to see what she could do to help Sally. After Christmas, things normally slowed down at the bed-and-breakfast, and she would have more time. She could cook meals, sit with Wilma, even help Sally with her shopping and more with the care, if she needed an entire day off. Whatever she needed, Lena would try to lend a hand.

She also wanted to keep an eye on Joe. Wintertime was his hardest time, because he couldn't always get out to fish. Fishing seemed to ease his mind and keep him grounded.

Winter also made it harder for his son to come up from Chicago to visit him.

Lena tried to keep that in mind as well.

"So did you foil her plans?" Lena asked, assuming that Sunday was there beside her because they'd gotten everything fixed and figured out.

"Actually no. She foiled her own plans, although not quite in the way that would have been beneficial to everyone involved."

"Okay?" Lena said, waiting patiently for Sunday to tell her the entire story.

"Well, it started out because Sally thought Norma Jean would be perfect for Peter. So she was going to kidnap Peter and then have Norma Jean go rescue him, expecting them both to get trapped in the shed by the storm. She even left them some blankets and food."

"What shed?"

"The shed on Peter's property. We used to play in it as children. I don't know if you know where it is?"

"It's the one where you guys stuck Clara in and then left her? And I ended up having to get her because you and your siblings forgot about her because your friends came in asking to go swimming and you totally forgot that you had your sister in the shed and she was stuck in the back room?"

That was pretty vivid in Lena's memories. Clara had been quite traumatized. Although, Clara had been happy once she had gotten out since she got to spend the rest of the day with her mother, and they'd gone out and taken a horseback ride together. One thing about having that many children, she didn't always get to spend one-on-one time with them, and when she did, it was usually cherished by both of them. That day was one of the best that she could remember having with Clara. After she got her out of the shed anyway.

"Exactly." Sunday looked around, and then her lips turned up in a smile as her eyes caught on something.

Lena figured it was Noah before she even turned her head and saw the man who was staring at her daughter, though he was in conversation with someone else.

"You were saying?" Lena prompted her when she realized that her daughter was caught on her husband and had totally forgotten she was in the middle of a story.

"Oh yeah. That's right. Anyway, Sally ended up taking the wrong man. She wasn't as familiar with Peter as she thought she was apparently, and she ended up taking Franklin."

"Franklin doesn't look anything like Peter. And Franklin usually has on some kind of business attire, while Peter is a lot more casual."

"Well, apparently Peter spilled a drink on Franklin, and Franklin borrowed his shirt. That's what Peter said anyway."

"So she didn't take Peter?"

"No. Peter's fine, and he thinks the whole thing is pretty funny."

"I bet he does, since he's not the one stuck in an unheated shed in the middle of a snowstorm," Lena said, wishing she could see outside. She didn't know whether it had started to snow or not.

"Anyway, Franklin had on Peter's shirt, and I guess Peter stuck his hat on his head too, and he says they have a very similar jaw outline. It was probably an understandable mistake. Especially considering that Sally has to be overtired and overworked."

"Being a caregiver is hard."

"That's what I've heard. Anyway, what ended up happening is Franklin got stuck out in the shed."

"Well, someone needs to go out and let him out then, is all I can think of," Lena said, thinking that was pretty straightforward. Even if it was starting to snow.

"That's the problem. Sally panicked, came running back, and sent Eleanor out to get Franklin."

"I see," Lena said, becoming more thoughtful. Eleanor, of all her children, was the most sensitive. A little bit on the quiet side and always thoughtful, she was the one who was least likely to get married. Lena had worried about her some, and then she had given her over to the Lord. It wasn't always in God's plan for people to get married. Maybe Eleanor was one of those people. She'd made it through her anxiety, and she had a deep, strong grounding in the Lord. Lena supposed that was really all a person needed.

Even if Lena did want to see her married, happily, with a family of her own.

"The last text Eleanor sent to me was that she was fine, everything was okay, and her phone was almost out of battery."

"And you haven't heard from her since?"

"I'm assuming her phone went dead."

"So you're assuming she's at the shack with Franklin?"

"Yes. I believe she was looking at a cat when she sent me the text. Which, Sally said there was a cat there that was pregnant, which is how she got Franklin to go out in the first place. She said she was in distress, although she wasn't. Anyway, I know that Eleanor made it out to get Franklin, but I don't know what happened after that. I wanted Ryan to go out and get them, but he just laughed and said that they would be fine."

Lena could see her son Ryan laughing over that. Ever since he'd come back from rodeo, he'd been not quite the same person.

Lena wasn't sure what to do to help him.

Still, that was a typical sibling reaction. Especially a brother.

"And no one else can go?"

"Noah's car doesn't go very well in the snow, and Matt and Luke and Davis have already told people that they would take them home from the dance if the snow started. They're going to be busy, and I hated to ask them. My car has bald tires, and I know that Eleanor's does too. We've been talking about how we needed to get tires on our vehicles, and we just haven't with all of the things that have been going on. My wedding and now this party have taken up all of our spare time."

Lena considered the situation. Part of her was worried for her daughter's safety. A Michigan snowstorm was nothing to sneeze at. Especially one like this, with lake-effect snow possibly dumping feet onto the ground, followed by a cold front.

People died in weather like this.

But her daughter was safe, had reached the shed, there was wood and a stove and the provisions that Sally had left.

"What are you thinking?" Lena finally said as Sunday continued to stand beside her.

"Well, I said something to you because... Honestly, I feel like we should just leave her there. I mean, Eleanor probably wouldn't be with Franklin on her own, and this might be good for her. Not that I want anything to happen to her. You know I love her more than life. But I think she'll be fine. Sally and Peter both said, when I questioned them separately, that the shack had been outfitted with wood and there was a stove. Peter said he had the stove cleaned, since he'd been planning on selling it. He hadn't done anything with the piles of firewood, which were stacked against the back of the shack. Sally said she had food and water and matches and blankets in the pack that she left. I... I feel like they're going to be okay. But I wanted to come talk to you. Because I can go get them if no one else can. Or Noah will. He'll do that first. I know he will if I ask him."

Lena nodded. Normally she wouldn't even consider leaving them there. But they would be fine, they had plenty of food, plenty of water, and plenty of wood for a fire. If she didn't think that Eleanor was perfectly capable of taking care of herself, she would be more concerned, but while Eleanor wasn't the most socially adept person, she was very scrappy and was very good at figuring out solutions to problems.

She had no fear for her life or her welfare.

And if they really wanted to get back, Eleanor could drive in the snow. Even with the bald tires.

She took a breath and blew it out. Knowing that if she made the wrong decision, she could regret it for the rest of her life.

Lord?

Sometimes God told her plainly what to do, and she didn't worry about making the wrong decision, but right now, she wasn't sure what decision was the best one, and she didn't feel any particularly strong guidance from the Lord.

She should have faith in her daughter, in her daughter's skills, and in her daughter's abilities.

"I think they'll be fine." She nodded, thinking to herself that she would drive out, just drive around, making sure that things were okay, before she came back.

She trusted her daughter, but she was also a mother, and while she believed that Eleanor would be okay, she'd feel a lot better if she made sure of it.

Still, she wouldn't mention that to Sunday, because then Sunday would insist that Noah drive, or she drive, and Lena could just slip out and do it on her own.

"That's what I thought too, but I just wanted to run it over with you. After all, Sally was going to leave Peter and Norma Jean there by themselves."

"Well, I definitely think that Sally needs to get out more. That was a crazy, harebrained scheme. And one that could have backfired in a big way, if she didn't make the proper preparations."

"She's just trying to help. She wants to be a blessing to people, and I think maybe she feels like she's stuck in the house with Miss Malone, changing bedpans and cooking vegetables and not really living life at all."

"But what she's doing is a blessing. Sometimes it's just hard to see it when it feels like only one person is benefiting."

"Plus, you grow a lot when you have to take care of someone else."

Lena nodded. Sunday sometimes was wise beyond her years. "It was a great party. I'm a little bit disappointed that Eleanor isn't here so I can congratulate her on it. She did an excellent job of organizing it."

"I didn't help her nearly as much as I wanted to. With the wedding and then just settling into married life, I just didn't find time. Eleanor didn't complain, and whenever people couldn't help her, she just went ahead and did it herself. If this is a success, she definitely deserves all the credit."

Lena nodded, glad that Sunday could give credit where it was due. Her children, perhaps because of her husband leaving, had grown up close to each other, without the typical jealousies and rivalries that siblings sometimes had.

Maybe that was another blessing of her husband leaving. She supposed the loneliness that she'd endured had been worth it. Worth the lessons her children had learned, the work ethics they had acquired, and the compassion for other people that they displayed.

If her husband hadn't left, maybe her children wouldn't have been like that.

"You know, Mom, you should probably consider yourself lucky that you aren't the one she was trying to kidnap. I've heard Sally saying that she needs to find a man for you." Sunday bumped her arm and winked before she strode off.

Lena didn't have a chance to reply, as she wasn't sure what she would say anyway.

Go ahead and kidnap me?

She chuckled to herself. No. She didn't want to have to sleep on the hard floor or be uncomfortable. After all, she passed fifty a few years ago, and her bones weren't as flexible as they used to be.

But maybe she wouldn't mind if someone wanted to match her up with someone.

That probably wasn't true. One thing about getting older, she had higher standards than she used to. She wasn't interested in just any old person. It wasn't even that she wanted to find someone who was perfectly compatible to her. That might have been more important when she was younger, but now, she wanted someone who had character and integrity. Who had a solid relationship with the Lord, and who wasn't easily offended. She didn't want to spend the rest of her life with someone she was always tiptoeing around trying not to make him angry.

She wanted someone who was going to love her the way she was. Not expect her to be a model on the cover of some magazine somewhere. She wanted someone who...thought about others more than they thought about themselves.

Where was she going to find such a paragon of virtue?

She laughed again. She probably wasn't going to find that. Any man who was like that had already been snatched up. Plus, she wasn't sure that she had matured to the point where she would be a good wife to someone like that. After all, if he was as good as she wanted him to be, he deserved a wife who was on his level, not someone like her, who still had so many rough edges that needed to be shaved off and filed so that she was more like Jesus.

She certainly had a tendency to think of herself more often than she should and to worry about things that she didn't need to. She got offended over things as well, although not like she used to when she was younger. And she had the baggage of having her husband cheat on her and leave.

Probably a person never really got over something like that, and it would be hard for her to trust again. She would want her husband to let her know where he was and what he was doing, and at her age, a man probably already was set in his ways and didn't want to have to answer to his wife for everything that he did. She wouldn't want there to be any secrets between them. Not on his computer, not on his phone, not on any piece of electronics. They would share passwords, they would know what each other was doing, at least in her perfect world.

Yeah, she was better off not being trapped with anyone. Her standards were way too high, and she would never find anyone who met even some of them. And she wasn't going to get married only to be miserable for the rest of her life.

She might as well be alone.

Chapter 12

F ranklin lay on the floor, not wanting to get up.

He'd dozed off and woken up twice to Eleanor crawling out or crawling back in bed after fixing the fire.

The last time it was fixed, he'd gotten up, and when he'd crawled back in, she turned over in her sleep, putting a leg over his and an arm around his waist, snuggling into his chest with a sigh.

He hadn't slept a wink after that.

And she was still there. After a little thought, he'd put his arm around her and tucked her in closer, putting his chin over top of her head and telling himself he enjoyed the warmth.

He enjoyed the feeling of closeness and companionship as well.

He would never have guessed that she was a person who had struggled with anxiety. She looked so calm and collected every time he'd seen her. Usually that was from afar, and often at the diner in Strawberry Sands.

Even when they'd been in high school, he wouldn't have thought that she had any issues.

Just goes to show that sometimes people's issues didn't manifest in ways that he would expect them to.

Still, he'd been running that over and over in his head, the thought that she'd decided that she was going to conquer it and she had. She was one determined person, who knew how to get things done. She might not be loud and might not seek a lot of attention, but she had a way of making things happen.

After all, she'd kept her business going while she planned the barn dance.

He'd no sooner thought that than an idea popped into his head: she could help him with his gala this weekend. She could be beside him, doing all of the things that Maisie usually did. She could organize the silent auction, mingle with guests, and just be there for him helping things run smoothly. As she had done this evening at the barn dance.

He didn't know why he hadn't thought of asking her last night. But the idea hadn't even crossed his mind when he had been telling her what his phone call had been about.

And now, the idea of trying to bring the subject up again and ask her if she'd go with him made his stomach twist and squirm. What if she said no?

Could he laugh it off?

After all, she'd asked him to dance, and he brushed her off, and somehow they'd made things work after they'd gotten stuck together.

Surely they could do the same thing with that. And it was a little bit of a challenge for him, if Eleanor could gather up the nerve to ask him, knowing that she had issues she had to overcome, surely he could gather up the nerve to see if she would go with him to the gala.

Of course, if she had been interested, she could have offered and she didn't.

He had to struggle to get past that. She wouldn't have thought to offer any more than he would have thought to ask her. A gala must be as foreign to her as a barn dance was to him.

She stirred, sighing a little, her arm tightening around him as her head nestled a little deeper. And then she froze.

He smiled. She must have woken up with a jolt, wondering where she was.

He resisted the urge to tighten his arm around her, to stroke her hair and tell her that it was okay, because it wasn't really his right to do that. They'd agreed to lie down together just because they needed each other's heat. It wasn't anything more than that, and for him to stroke her hair or hold her close seemed to cross a line that he hadn't realized he was close to.

Her arm slid from around his waist, and her body moved back a fraction of an inch.

He grinned a little, and then he said, "I'm awake. It's okay. You rolled over the last time I got out and came back again, and it was actually nice because your leg over top of mine is keeping me warm."

She jerked, and her leg snapped off his, and this time, her whole body jerked back too, taking the blanket with it.

"And now my back is cold." He added that in the same tone he'd been talking to her in, just a casual, everything is a-okay kind of tone.

"Oh my goodness. I'm so embarrassed. I'm sorry. I had no idea I was practically plastered to you."

She ducked her head, and he could imagine that her cheeks were a cute color of pink.

"It's getting light out. It's still snowing. At least it was when I was up. I opened the door to check."

"The cat?" she asked, lifting her head up to look into the far corner.

"She was sleeping with her kittens. I ran my hand over them, and they all felt warm."

"That's good to know," she said on a sigh.

It was getting slightly lighter, although it probably would never be like daylight inside the cabin since there were only two windows. And today would be darker than normal days, because of the snow and the clouds.

"I think this was supposed to stop by dinnertime."

"I think it was. I heard a couple of cars, so the road must be passable, but nobody stopped. I think, if we really needed to, we could have gone out and stood by the road and flagged someone down."

"A snowplow at the very least. I heard a couple of those go by."

"Me too. Maybe that's why no one is really concerned about us. But it's comforting to know if it had been absolutely necessary, we could have gotten ourselves out of here."

"I'm happy with our decision to stay though. I hope you don't regret it. I really am sorry for throwing myself at you."

"You didn't. And you might have missed it, but my arm was around you too. It was warmer that way."

"All right. I guess I'm still a bit embarrassed, but if you insist."

"I do." He took a breath. "Before we get started with the things that we need to do," he said, thinking that they needed to bring more wood in, they needed to go outside and use the restroom, and he was hungry as well and thirsty, "I wanted to ask you something."

"Okay?" she said, sounding a little bit more awake and relaxed. Like she'd accepted the fact that it wasn't her fault that they'd ended up snuggled up together.

"Do you remember the phone call I told you about, and the gala I talked about, and how I don't have a date for it?"

"Yeah?"

He realized his heart was beating fast and his hands had started to sweat. He really cared about her answer.

"Would you be interested in going with me?"

Chapter 13

Eleanor looked at him with her mouth hanging wide open.

"You organized everything last night. You'd do a great job there, I'm sure of it."

Oh. That changed things. He just wanted her because she was good at organizing things. For a minute there, she was thinking he was asking her out on a date. That he liked her, that maybe he was feeling some of the same feelings she was.

She should have known better. He just wanted somebody to help him, and she was a good candidate.

But she could. And she would enjoy it. It would be a chance to get out, and she could be friends with Franklin. Maybe she was feeling like she wanted something more, but if friends was all he wanted, she could do that.

"Don't feel like you have to. Chicago is a little different than Strawberry Sands,"

She laughed. "I think I know that. And I suppose ten years ago, this would have terrified me. But I actually think it might be fun."

"It might be the kind of thing that you enjoy. Some people do. I like having done it, but I don't usually like the planning or the execution. But after it's over, I always have a great feeling of satisfaction. Mostly because we raise a lot of money for a good cause."

"The Chicago Midtown Humane Society?"

He nodded.

Humane societies were close to her heart as well. Obviously, considering that she was a dog groomer by trade, animals were a big part of her life.

"When is it again?" she asked, hedging a little bit. It wasn't that she didn't want to. She just thought that maybe he could find someone who would be better for him. She didn't want to hold him back when someone else would help him rather than hinder him. And while she was pretty sure she would have a great time, with her inexperience, she was afraid she might not be a great help.

"It's Saturday night. Tomorrow."

"Wow. I need to get a dress."

He smiled and shrugged. "I never even thought about it, but I suppose you probably would."

She had no idea what to wear. She'd never been to anything remotely like a big gala in Chicago. Hadn't been interested.

"Is there anything I need to do in the meantime?"

"No. When we're there, there is a little bit of mingling and keeping track of things. We've switched to an online auction, so it's not quite as difficult as it was, but there are still some hands-on things that you just can't give to a machine to do."

"I see."

"Seriously, I'd love to have you, but I don't want you to feel obligated or anxious."

"I don't feel obligated. I would like to help you. I... I was kinda thinking that maybe we're friends now." She said that a little tentatively. After all, she had been thinking that she would like to be more, and she'd been way off the mark with that. Maybe he was still thinking of them as barely acquaintances; even though they did spend so much time together, it was just for one day.

"Yeah. I definitely thought we were friends." He lifted his shoulder. "I didn't think we had to quantify that, but you can't really go through something like this with someone and not come out on the other side feeling like you know them a little better. And, I have to say, I was not disappointed in you."

Well, that wasn't exactly an undying declaration of love, but not being disappointed was probably a good thing.

Rather than trying to figure out what their relationship was, she lifted her chin and looked him in the eye. "I'll go. I'll get a dress somehow, if we get rescued. And just tell me where I need to meet you in Chicago."

"When we get our phones back, I'll text you the address of the gala, but maybe I can pick you up so we can ride together."

"I wouldn't expect you to come the whole way up to Strawberry Sands to pick me up, and I'm assuming you're going back to Chicago as soon as we get...rescued." She said that a little bit ironically, since she did have a car outside. "Maybe I can try my car if the snow lets up."

"Maybe, although there's no shovel around, and we'd probably need to shovel you out."

"Yeah, I don't think it's going to quite go through all the snow to get to the road. But I think the road will be clear shortly after the snow stops. They're usually really good about it."

"I'm going to go out and get a few more loads of firewood."

"That sounds good. I'll get the bread and meat and make us some sandwiches. If you're hungry?"

He pushed the blankets off and got up, holding out a hand for her. She took it and pulled herself up, trying not to pay attention to how his hand felt holding hers.

"I'm definitely hungry. Although, if we have sandwiches all day, plus the sandwich that I had last night, I'm probably going to be ready for something other than sandwiches tomorrow."

"Me too, although if we spend too much more time here, I guess I'll just be happy for anything to eat, because we probably have enough to last us today, but not anymore."

"Hopefully Sally remembers that she only provided enough food for two days. And doesn't leave us stranded out here any longer than that."

They laughed a little together before he went outside.

She started putting the sandwiches together, thinking while she did so. She'd never been to a gala, but that didn't mean that she couldn't go. That she couldn't learn. She could. It would be a great experience, and who knew, maybe she'd learn something new, or it would open a door to something else.

She tried to focus on those thoughts and not on the nervousness she felt. She didn't want to embarrass him, cause him any trouble, or make things more difficult for him. And she was afraid that was what she was going to do.

The two sides warred in her head as he came back in with an armful of wood, then went back out for another one after telling her that the roads were clear and it looked like the snow stopped.

Good news. Really good news, except... She didn't really mind being stranded with him. He admitted almost as much to her, too.

She had both sandwiches ready by the time he came in with another load of firewood. After ducking back outside to wash his hands in the snow, he came back in and she handed him a sandwich.

Bowing her head, she said a short prayer, thanking God that they were fine last night, that they were able to start a fire, that there was food, and that she'd been stuck with someone who had a good head on his shoulders, instead of someone who would have panicked. All things that she'd been silently thanking God for in short bullet prayers since she'd woken up.

"You can just say that out loud for both of us, or if you want me to?" His words interrupted her.

"I didn't want to push on you if it wasn't something you did." She looked at her sandwich and then looked back up at him. "I know we're stuck here in a shack, and there are a lot of things that we could say went wrong, but I'm just so grateful for all the things that went right. Having food, being able to start a fire, the fact that the cat had the rest of her kittens without any more trouble, and you. I'm thankful for you. It would have been terrible to be stuck here with someone who complained the entire time or even worse to be stuck with someone who was scared to death and panicked."

"I could say the exact same thing. I've been thinking over and over this morning how grateful I am that it was you that I was stuck with. I can think of a lot of people, male and female, who wouldn't have been nearly as reasonable and...fun. It's been fun."

She laughed. "I was thinking the same thing, I think we talked about that a little bit last night, and this morning too. On the one hand, I want to get out of here. I haven't been without my phone for such a long time in forever. It's...a little bit of withdrawal. I want to make sure everyone is okay, and I want them to know that I'm okay. But beyond that, I feel like I could stay here for a really long time and be perfectly happy."

"There's just a total lack of pressure or any kind of worry or fear. I'm not even concerned about people coming to get us. Someone will be here eventually."

"If I were you, I might be a little concerned about whether or not I'm going to make it to my gala."

"The thought has crossed my mind, but I know we're not going to be here that long. I also know that I have people in charge of making sure everything is ready. The only thing

I have to do is show up and take charge of the silent auction. I've done it so much that I'm not worried about it at all."

They ate their sandwiches, then he added more wood to the fire and she fed the cat. As far as she could tell, the kittens were doing well and the mama seemed fine. He walked over after he was done fueling the fire and crouched down beside her.

"She's purring just as loud as she can. You couldn't tell that she was in such distress yesterday."

"And the kitten seems to be fine too. I guess that's one more thing to be thankful for."

He nodded, and the look he gave her was a little bit thoughtful, even though there was a smile tripping up his lips.

They walked over to the stove, sitting down in front of it and sharing blankets and talking about different things, nothing deep or personal like they had the night before. It seemed like in the daylight, they agreed to keep the topics superficial.

They heard the snowplow going back and forth several times, and Eleanor had to admit that she was disappointed when a rumbling noise seemed to stop in front of the shack and then come up the driveway.

"Sounds like our rescuers are here." Franklin tilted his head and then heaved out a sigh. "I suppose we should get up and greet them. Is that what you do when you've been abducted and are being kept in a shack? Is it polite to greet newcomers?"

"I'm not sure I've ever learned the etiquette on that situation exactly," Eleanor said, and the smile they shared was rather bittersweet. She understood that he was just as reluctant as she was to admit that their time was over. But it was probably for the best. He had a gala to attend, and so did she.

Not to mention, she had a dress to buy.

With that thought, she scrambled up beside him and awaited their rescue.

Chapter 14

"Thanks again," Franklin said as he got out of Matt Landry's plow truck. Eleanor's brother Matt had been the one to rescue them. He had chatted with them and admitted that he'd gotten all his plowing done before he'd come and said he wasn't in that big of a hurry to get them, and Franklin got the feeling that it was because he was hoping that Eleanor might actually find herself a match.

It made Franklin a little bit sad for Eleanor, since her family seemed to think that she couldn't find someone on her own.

Regardless, Matt also had his phone, and Franklin was eager to get into his hotel and up to his room in order to charge it.

He nodded at the front desk clerk and continued to the elevators as he walked through, scanning the area to make sure everything was okay.

He and Noah didn't make a whole lot of visits to the hotel on official business. Noah had moved to Strawberry Sands, and the house that he had been building was finished.

So he saw the outside of the hotel at least pretty much every day.

Franklin, on the other hand, had a little bit more trouble deciding that he really wanted to leave Chicago.

Of course, last night, first the barn dance, and then being stuck with Eleanor, hadn't been terrible. He wouldn't have had nearly as much fun doing anything in Chicago. Even though most people would not have considered last night to be a good time.

Franklin still couldn't quite get over the fact that he did.

He punched the numbers in the elevator and waited for it to take him up to his floor where he kept a room available for any time he was in town.

He went into his room and plugged his phone in right away. After that, he took a shower, using the spare clothes that he kept packed for such emergencies.

He laughed at the thought. He hadn't packed any clothes thinking that he was going to be abducted and spend the night in a shack while a major snowstorm raged around him.

Or that he would need a plow truck in order to be rescued.

Matt had let Eleanor off first, and Franklin had promised to send her the information of where to meet him in Chicago. She had insisted that it wouldn't be a problem to meet him there, since she needed to get a dress anyway. She assured him that her sister Sunday would probably go with her.

She actually seemed excited. He smiled at the thought. Honestly, he was a little excited. For the gala, sure. It was the highlight of the year for his company. And he loved it. It was always a good time, and he really enjoyed the feeling of raising money for a good cause.

But beyond that, he had to admit that there was a special excitement in his chest, and it had everything to do with Eleanor. Going with Maisie had never made his pulse race or his mind churn with possibilities. In fact, he often counted down the minutes until he could thank her and get away. She was a nice woman, and he admired her. He respected her as a business associate and considered her a friend, but the thought of being with her didn't make his chest warm, make him smile, make him think of all the things that he admired about her. They got along okay, but he was always happy to part at the end of the night. He never felt like he wanted to spend more time with her or that he just didn't get enough.

But that was the way he felt with Eleanor. Disappointed that the tow truck came, wishing they had another night together. Not necessarily so that they could snuggle up, although he hadn't minded that at all. But more so that they could continue to talk. She was funny and smart without being arrogant or a know-it-all.

She was easy to talk to, and she was interested in a lot of the same things he was.

He put his clean clothes on, hung his towel up, and walked out of the bathroom.

He should have known there would be a hundred messages on his phone.

It was ringing as he reached for it, and he saw it was Noah, his business partner and Eleanor's brother-in-law. Suddenly, he wanted to ask Noah a thousand questions about Eleanor. But he held his tongue, swiped his phone, and said, "Hello?"

"Hey, man. So how was it?"

"How was what?" he asked, smirking and playing dumb.

"Being trapped in a shack with my sister-in-law. I can't think of a worse fate."

"Your sister-in-law's pretty nice. Being trapped wasn't the best, but... I'm not too upset about it. I could stay longer. As long as we didn't run out of food, I was good."

"You're kidding. Mr. 'I can't leave Chicago because I love the city' was happy being trapped in a shack in the middle of nowhere during the snowstorm?"

"Yeah. I was fine." He shrugged a shoulder, walking over and standing in front of the window looking out at the parking lot. The snow had been plowed off it, cinders had been thrown down, and big piles of snow heaped up on either side.

The lot itself was mostly empty, which was totally normal for this time of day.

"I'm in shock. I thought you'd be complaining up a storm."

He laughed at Noah's choice of words. "Why? There is no point in complaining. And it really wasn't that bad. I actually enjoyed spending a dozen hours or so without my phone. I should do that more often."

"You could turn it off and walk away from it. You don't have to go quite to that extreme."

"I know." He didn't want to say anything more about Eleanor, and he was hoping Noah would let it go.

"It must've been the company. I'm going to have to call Eleanor. Sunday," he said to his wife, "you should get her on the phone."

"Actually, she probably will be calling Sunday just as soon as she can. She's going to the gala with me tomorrow."

"What?" Noah's surprise came through the phone loud and clear. "What about Maisie? You didn't dump her, did you?"

"No. I can hardly dump her. We're not exactly a couple."

"Everybody knows you go places together. We were just waiting for you guys to actually get together-together. You know she's in love with you."

"No, she's not. She feels the exact same way about me that I feel about her. Someone to go places with, someone uncomplicated, with no drama."

"That's what you want to think," Noah mumbled.

"That's what I know. Plus, her sister has malaria, and she was dropping everything and going to Africa. I had to find someone else, and...I ended up stuck with your sister. She happens to be a dog groomer and is interested in the humane society, and she was willing to help me out. Plus, she did a great job on the barn dance."

"She actually did do a great job on the barn dance. And she ended up doing most of it herself. She hangs in there and gets things done. You can definitely consider Eleanor dependable. I... I'm a little surprised though that she agreed to go to the gala with you."

Franklin paused. Then he said slowly, "Because of her anxiety?"

"Did she tell you about that?" Noah asked, sounding even more surprised than he had when Franklin told him Eleanor was going.

"She did. Why do you sound so surprised about it?"

"Because she doesn't tell anyone. No one knows. No one except family."

"Well, then maybe I'm family." He wanted to know what Noah thought about it. What Sunday had told him, since he assumed it was Sunday who said something. But he didn't ask. Eleanor had worked so hard to get over it, he kind of hated the thought that she was defined by it. But he supposed that a person's past helped shape their reputation, and there really wasn't anything a person could do about it.

Noah laughed like he was joking. And Franklin didn't bother to try to do anything to correct him.

They chatted for a bit more before Noah hung up, and Franklin swiped off as well.

Noah hadn't said much about Eleanor, and Franklin hadn't wanted to push it, because he didn't want Noah to know how interested he was. It might turn out to be nothing, and he didn't want to be hearing about it from now until doomsday if it did. And he didn't want a big deal made out of it, to make things uncomfortable anytime he would see her in the future.

He texted her the address of the gala. He really wanted to pick her up, but he was going to be busy all day getting things ready, and he knew it was probably best that he didn't. Noah would see that she got there okay. Franklin grinned. He couldn't wait to see her again, and not just at the gala.

Because he would be seeing her. Not just because Noah was married to her sister Sunday, and Noah was his business partner, but because Franklin was going to make sure of it.

He was still smiling as he brought his phone down and started scrolling through his messages. It took a few minutes to check to see that there was nothing pressing, and then he went to his voicemails and started listening.

The second one was from Maisie.

"Hey, Franklin. Sorry to bother you again, but my sister just called me back. Our connection wasn't that great, but she told me not to bother to come, that they had misdiagnosed her with malaria, when she was actually just dehydrated. I guess when they took her temperature the first time, no one shook the thermometer down, and they read 105 degrees, when she actually didn't have a fever at all.

"Anyway, she got some fluids, and she's home now. She is going to be able to make her plane, and she'll be here for Christmas like we planned. I'm sorry for the back-and-forth, but I wanted to call you as soon as possible and let you know that I'm still on for the gala.

"All right, not sure where you are that you're not answering, that's kind of unusual, but I'll see you tomorrow, when the city plows out from the latest snow. Oh, the joys of living in Chicagoland." He could hear the eye roll in her voice before she hung up.

Oh boy. Now what?

He held the phone without really noticing it was in his hand as he stared at the wall, trying to figure out what in the world to do.

What was the right thing?

He knew what he wanted to do. He wanted to call Maisie back immediately and tell her not to worry about it, that he was going with someone else. But if Maisie was available, that's who he always went with. They had an understanding. She expected to be with him.

But he had asked Eleanor. Eleanor had said yes, and Eleanor was expecting to go with him.

What was he going to do? He wasn't sure.

One thing he knew for certain was that he couldn't go with two women. He was going to have to tell one of them that he didn't need her. But he couldn't figure out which one to tell.

He didn't want to hurt either of their feelings, as a human, but as a man, Eleanor was the one that he wanted to keep happy. To make happy. To spend time with, to see her smile. To protect her. He had a fierce desire to protect her. He couldn't believe how that had reared its head while they had been stranded together.

But more than that, he just wanted to spend time with her. And if he told her that he didn't need her anymore, that Maisie was able to go after all, was she going to understand?

He didn't think she would necessarily be angry, but he did think that her feelings might be hurt, and she might not be interested in going anywhere with him again. That was a risk he really didn't want to take.

He dialed Maisie's number.

Unfortunately, she didn't answer. He thought about leaving a message but decided that that was something that he wanted to tell her face-to-face. If he did have to cancel, he didn't want to hurt her feelings either. If things didn't work out between Eleanor and him, and even if they did, he didn't want to ruin the friendship that he had with Maisie.

As he ran through his other messages, he saw several that he needed to respond to immediately, and he realized that some of the information he needed was on his laptop in Chicago.

He had planned to stick around Strawberry Sands, maybe see if Eleanor wanted to go to the diner to have supper, but he should have known that, while he hired a company to take care of all of the planning and execution of the gala, there were a lot of things that he needed to handle as well. He didn't know why he forgot that from year to year.

He grabbed his things, including his dirty clothes, and walked out to the parking lot, scraping the snow off his car and heading toward Chicago.

He would talk to Maisie first, make sure everything was smooth with her, and then he would see what he could do with Eleanor.

It was funny, he was someone who had not spent much time with women at all, in fact had a friend to work as his date anytime he needed her, and now he had two women for one situation. It was an awkward place to be.

Chapter 15

"I really appreciate you coming with me," Eleanor said to Sunday as she waited in line to pay for the dress they had found in Chicago.

The snowstorm had stopped, the roads were clear, and Eleanor decided that she wasn't going to wait.

She should talk to Sally, give her a hard time, but she couldn't find it in her heart to do that.

So, she settled the cat in her home, asked her sister Clara to make sure she got fed overnight and the next day, and then she and Sunday took off for Chicago.

They made it to this boutique in plenty of time for her to try on a few things. The price tags had made her feel faint, but they found a nice dark green, almost black, velvet dress on the clearance rack, which, when coupled with a cute jacket, would look very nice. She had her black high-heeled boots that were dressy enough to wear with it, and Sunday had told her that she had the perfect necklace to go along with it.

Even the clearance price had been more than Eleanor had ever thought she would pay for a dress. It was enough to pay for the snow tires for her car.

Because she'd been saving for the tires, she had the money in her account, and she only cringed a little as the clerk rang up her purchase and charged her card.

"Like I would miss a shopping trip to Chicago," Sunday said. She put her arm around Eleanor as the clerk smiled and handed her card back. "Plus, you were awesome in my wedding. Not only did you help me, but you made Hope look beautiful as well. How could I turn you down?"

"Easily. You just got married, we just had a snowstorm, and Chicago is the last place that either one of us wants to be."

That might not be entirely true. Eleanor would be a lot more excited about being in Chicago if she thought that Franklin was there too. But he said he was going to stay at the hotel and do a little work, and then drive up tomorrow morning in time to be at the convention center to oversee the final preparations for the gala.

"Oh my goodness. I didn't see that!" Sunday said, hurrying over to a rack where they had their spring collection out already.

Eleanor knew those clothes would be way out of her price range, and she walked over slower, the dress that she just purchased in one hand, while she slipped her card back in her wallet with the other.

Her phone rang.

She shoved her wallet under her arm and pulled her phone out of her pocket, swiping and sticking it to her ear without glancing at the id.

"Hello?"

"Eleanor. Hey."

"Franklin. I... It's only been a couple of hours. Do you miss me already?" She was just goofing with him. Maybe trying to cover the surprise that he called her so soon.

Maybe he thought of something he needed to tell her about the gala.

"Do you have some last-minute instructions for me?"

"No. Not really."

"All right. I just finished buying my dress. It was on clearance, so I'm committed since I can't take it back, although I just paid more for it than I would have paid for my snow tires. But Sunday assures me that I look amazing in it, so it was worth the money."

"You just bought the dress? And you can't take it back?" He didn't sound overly thrilled about it.

"Yes." She tried not to let his odd tone discourage her. He was probably swamped with things to do now that they weren't trapped anymore. "And a little jacket to go with it. It's really cute."

She closed her mouth. Her brothers were never interested in what her clothes looked like. She assumed Franklin probably wasn't either, even though she wanted to talk about it. After all, he didn't sound excited, and she was hoping that she hadn't gone and done something wrong. She said that she got it off the clearance rack. Surely it was okay to wear a dress to the gala that a person had bought on clearance? Most of the Christmas dresses were on clearance.

"Are you sure you can't take it back?"

"No. That's okay. I mean, I've never spent that much on a dress in my life before, but it's for a good cause, right?"

Maybe she should stop talking about money. Maybe that's what was so awful. Maybe Franklin was from the kind of family who didn't discuss finances.

She'd grown up in a family that talked about them pretty much every day. Mostly because her mom was a single mom, and the kids were all very aware that they all needed to pitch in so that they could stay on the farm and survive.

Her mom had never tried to hide any of that from them, which Eleanor had thought was a good thing. It helped them all want to do their best to help make money, and it made them proud of themselves when they made the mortgage payment every month.

But she knew that not all families were like hers, and some really cringed at the mention of anything having to do with finances or money.

And maybe it was too personal, even though she felt like she and Franklin really were friends, since they'd been stuck together, and that had a tendency to bond people, but maybe she didn't know as much about him as what she thought.

"Yeah. I guess you can spend as much money as you want to on a dress..." He sounded depressed.

"Is everything okay?" She stopped, staring at the rack and her sister's back but not really seeing them. There was something wrong. She might not know him very well, but she could tell that for sure.

"Actually, there is a problem."

"What's up?"

"Remember I told you about Maisie?"

"Yes. Her sister had malaria—did she pass away?" Eleanor's hand went to her throat. "Oh, that's terrible! Do you need to help her? Do you need to go to Africa?" She couldn't imagine that he actually did, but maybe he and Maisie were great friends, and he wanted to be there for her during this difficult time. "If you do, that's fine. I can...put the dress away and maybe wear it some other time." She couldn't take it back. Even though she hadn't even set foot out of the store, the clearance sign clearly said that all clearance sales were final.

"No. Nothing like that. She's... She's actually better. It was a...false alarm. The... Her fever wasn't as bad as what they thought it was, and it turned out that she just had a little bit of dehydration, I guess."

"That's awesome. I'm so glad. My goodness, I'm sure Maisie is relieved."

"Yeah. She is. And...she's not going to Africa anymore."

Eleanor froze. Oh. That was what this call was about. He didn't need her anymore. He had Maisie again.

"Okay. Well, I see. So Maisie is able to go to the gala with you?" She tried to infuse her typical cheerfulness back into her voice. And really, this made sense. Maisie had been the one to be his dependable date for years. He hadn't said for how long, but they had an understanding. He wouldn't want to turn her down and mess that up. He would want to take her if he could. Of course.

"I was just a stand-in, now you don't need me anymore. That's fine."

"It's not like that." He said that quickly, which just made Eleanor's eyes draw down.

"It's not like that?" she asked. "So you aren't calling to tell me that you don't need me to go to the gala with you anymore?" Did she totally misunderstand something?

"No. That's what I wanted to say." His voice still sounded like he didn't want to say what he was saying, but he had to. "I just wanted to let you know about Maisie. I wasn't going to go with her if it was going to upset you. I mean, she's expecting to go with me and everything, but...it's business."

Upset her? He'd told her he was going with her and now just...wanted to let her know about Maisie? Why else would he tell her about Maisie unless he wanted her to tell him it was okay for him to go with her? Her chest felt tight and hot, but she tried to ignore it and be kind, to make this as easy as possible for him. After all, wasn't that what she was supposed to do? Think of others over herself? Here was an opportunity to try to put Franklin first and herself last, as much as she wanted to be short or unkind.

"You don't need to call it anything other than what it is. It's okay. I'm a big girl, and I can understand that. You definitely want to keep the good thing going that you have with Maisie. She's been faithful and dependable for years. It would be wrong of you to have to tell her that you're going with someone else. Plus, she knows everything she needs to do to help you."

"I didn't think you'd have a dress already."

Of course she was going to have a dress. That was the first thing she thought of when he asked her to go. The gala was the next day. She wasn't going to go any longer than what she had to without purchasing something.

Except now of course, she wished she would have waited.

She wished she would have bought the snow tires.

She laughed a little. Always practical. Maisie probably was not practical. Or maybe she was. It didn't matter. She had a dress she didn't need instead of snow tires which she did.

Maybe she could find a place to wear it.

"That's okay. Sunday is here in Chicago with me, and we were already planning on staying overnight in a hotel. Maybe we can find…a show or something to attend." She didn't want to go to the gala. Not with Franklin going with someone else. That would be hard enough to watch. Seeing him with someone else. Not that she was in love with him or anything, but she definitely liked him. More than she should obviously, since this bothered her more than she thought it would.

"You can still come."

"Probably not though. Thanks anyway."

She didn't know what else to say. She'd never had this happen to her before. Where some guy asked her to go somewhere and then decided to go with someone else. She knew it wasn't quite like that. Franklin's relationship with Maisie was a little bit more complicated and definitely predated her own relationship with him.

"I appreciate your loyalty. Even if it's not directed at me, I appreciate the fact that you're loyal. I like that." There. That was true. She truly did appreciate loyalty, and Franklin was displaying it currently. If she were Maisie, she would definitely admire it.

"I… I didn't want to call you."

"I'm sure it was an awkward situation to be in, and I can appreciate the fact that this was a difficult phone call. Was there anything else you needed?" She knew she probably shouldn't ask that last question. But she wanted to get off the phone. She didn't want to talk to him anymore. She just wanted to go and…process things. Not with Franklin and not by speaking, because she didn't want to say something that might hurt him. It wasn't her desire to hurt him. Even though her heart hurt. Not that he'd even done it on purpose. She knew truly that he hadn't. He made the best decision that he could. She knew that for sure, but it didn't make it hurt her less.

"Seriously. I... I would like to go out with you. Would you be interested?"

She wasn't sure what he was saying.

"Not to the gala," she clarified, just to make sure. She wasn't the slightest bit interested in going with someone who was already with someone. To be the second woman on his arm? No thank you. No way.

"No," he said quickly. "Some other time. Maybe... We can find somewhere to go where you can wear that dress. I can reimburse you for it," he added, like he just thought of that.

"I don't think so." She liked him. She liked him a lot. But even while she admired his loyalty and admired the fact that he was being loyal to a friend who was older than she was and who had been friends with him longer than she had, she couldn't escape the fact that she was his second choice. She didn't want to be with someone where she was his second choice. She didn't particularly want to be alone and didn't like being single, but she wasn't so desperate to have a significant other that she would accept being second.

"I think it's probably better if we just let it go."

She didn't want to say that. She wanted to say yes. But she knew she was making the right decision. If she allowed him to put her in second place now and went out with him anyway, maybe he would think that she would always accept second place.

She wasn't sure if that logic made any sense at all, but God could have worked it out completely differently, and He didn't. Maybe when she had time to think about it, she'd figure out that God was saying something else, but for right now, it seemed like the good Lord was letting her know that this wasn't something that was meant to be.

It wasn't exactly the information that she wanted, but she felt like she was saying the right thing.

"I see," Franklin said, but he didn't sound happy.

"Hey, I hope everything goes really well tomorrow night. I hope you have a lot of fun, and you know I'm really pulling for you guys to make a lot of money on your auction. Let me know how much, okay?"

"I'm sure you'll see it on the news. But yeah. I'll let you know."

They hung up shortly after, and Eleanor just stood there in the store. Shoppers walked around her, and Sunday was deep in discussion with one of the sales ladies, who was trying to talk her into trying on a dress. It looked like an expensive one to Eleanor, but she honestly didn't care. Sunday normally wouldn't have any need to wear a dress like that, but now that she was married to Noah, it probably was good for her to expand her wardrobe, and maybe that was why she eagerly accepted Eleanor's invitation to go shopping in Chicago.

Their differences had never been more stark. And even though Eleanor knew when Sunday married Noah that her life was going to change, the changes hadn't been obvious to Eleanor until just now.

Sunday had money. She could buy dresses, and go to galas, and do all kinds of things that they only dreamed about when they were little girls.

And Eleanor was completely happy for her. Truly she was.

The only thing she was a little bit jealous about was the fact that Sunday had a husband who doted on her. She wasn't second in her husband's eyes.

And that made all the difference to Eleanor.

Regardless, she walked over, and Sunday did indeed try on the dress, plus two more, and ended up buying one of them.

It was an hour later, and Eleanor was trying not to show how badly she wanted to go home and cuddle up with her cat or just be alone, when Sunday suggested that they go to the coffee shop across the street to grab a bite to eat before they went to their hotel.

Eleanor hadn't told her what the phone call had been about, and Sunday had been too busy looking at the dresses to ask.

But they were in Chicago, they already had a hotel booked, and they might as well enjoy their time. Eleanor decided that once they got their food and sat down, she'd break the news to Sunday and then ask her if she thought there were any shows in town that they might attend while they were there. They might as well wear their new clothes and enjoy themselves, since that's what they had set out to do.

Chapter 16

"We'll make do. If they sent roses instead of carnations, we'll use roses," Franklin said, thinking that it was common sense but understanding why Lynette, head of the PR firm he hired to oversee the charity gala, wanted to know. After all, he gave her parameters, and part of the parameters was having carnations.

"All right. I'll make it work. Did you get my message about the door prizes?"

"I did, and it's okay," he said, referring to the prizes that she had texted him. All were as he had wanted except for one, where she couldn't find the exact type of plant he suggested, and substituted.

It was fine. The important thing was that they had door prizes and that they were the kind of prizes that would be acceptable to the type of people who would be there.

"I'll call you if I need anything else."

"That's fine. I'm in Chicago. I hadn't planned to be, but after I meet with a few associates, I'll be stopping in."

"All right. I have a few things I want to run by you. I was going to wait until tomorrow morning, but we can get them settled now." Her voice changed as she called out, "No! Don't put the tree there. It goes over on the other side. It's going to balance the one on that side. See?" She lowered her voice again and said into her phone, "I need to go."

"All right."

They hung up, and Franklin stood in the street, just a block or so down from the office he had in downtown Chicago.

There was a cute little coffee shop as well as other various shops along the sidewalk. It was a place he often saw tourists, but office workers from downtown were close enough to walk to it as well.

It's where Maisie had wanted to meet.

His phone call with her hadn't gone the way he wanted it to, and he couldn't find it in his heart to tell her that everything she had assumed was wrong.

Plus, she had been so happy that her sister was well and so excited that she didn't have to go to Africa. And she was brimming with ideas for the silent auction, had asked to meet so they could run over some of those things.

She also wanted to show him the dress she bought, which he didn't care about, but he hadn't told her no.

When she said that she bought a dress, and that she had a bunch of ideas, and that she wanted to meet, he decided he wasn't going to let her down and that he would call Eleanor instead.

How ironic was it that Eleanor had been buying a dress as he'd been talking to Maisie about it? She had to have been, if she had just purchased it right before he called as she said.

He thought it was ironic that they had apparently been heading to Chicago at about the same time. She hadn't known he was going, because he had planned to stay in Strawberry Sands. He hadn't known that she was going because she hadn't told him, although she had mentioned she needed a dress. Maybe she was waiting to see what time would suit her sister to go with her.

Regardless, it was just the way the timing had worked out.

Almost as though God was trying to show that he made the wrong decision.

There wasn't anything he could do now. He'd already muddled things up so much that he felt like he just needed to walk forward. Trying to turn Maisie down at this point and then talking Eleanor into going with him would be a lot of time and effort especially since he'd already not treated her well, and he was getting down to the wire. He could go from having two women ready to go with him to having none.

But honestly, having a date for the gala wasn't the important thing.

He'd been a lot more let down than what he expected when Eleanor wasn't interested in going anywhere else with him and had turned down his invitation to do something at some point. It was a broad invitation, on purpose, because he just wanted to get a yes out of her, but he hadn't been successful.

He walked slowly, because he knew he was early. He'd left the office way before he needed to just because he was having trouble focusing.

He got his work finished but couldn't think of anything else to do. Even though he knew there was plenty.

The sidewalks had been plowed, the Christmas lights hung on the streetlights, and people carried packages and steaming Styrofoam cups filled with coffee and hot chocolate. He could smell both on the air.

"Franklin!"

He turned, realizing he was almost at the coffee shop where they had agreed to meet.

Normally, he and Maisie were very, if not formal, reserved. But maybe it was because Maisie was so relieved about her sister, or maybe it was just the Christmas season, because instead of greeting him with a handshake or a head nod like she might normally do, she hurried to him and threw her arms around him.

He turned his face and realized if he hadn't, her lips would have pressed against his. As it was, they hit his cheek. He was too surprised to do anything more than hug her back and wonder what in the world was going on.

He absentmindedly patted her back, thinking that just the night before he had been holding Eleanor. Eleanor felt different. Curvier maybe. A little less slender, but somehow she felt right. Where Maisie didn't.

He stared off across the street, waiting for Maisie to pull back, not wanting to jerk away from her, as his instinct had wanted him to do.

As he did, his eyes suddenly focused on a woman who stared at him.

The woman wore a cheerful bright red coat and had a cream-colored beanie on her head. Her cheeks were rosy, and her eyes glowed, but as he watched, her smile faded.

Her eyes were on him. Maisie had started to pull back as he recognized the woman.

Eleanor.

Eleanor, of course. She was shopping in Chicago. This was a popular spot for tourists, and of course she was shopping here. He'd never even thought to ask, but it made sense. Total sense.

"Oh my goodness. You cannot believe how relieved I am. And how happy I am to not miss the gala. It was so hard for me to make that phone call. But you made it easy for me of course. You always do. You're so understanding." Maisie had backed up, but her hands had slid down his arms and her mitten hands had clasped his.

She squeezed his fingers now, and he jerked his eyes to her, realizing what she was saying and wondering what in the world he was going to say in return.

She'd kissed him. Hugged him, and now she was holding his hands. Eleanor had seen it all.

He hadn't meant anything by it, but if he had seen some man do that to Eleanor, he would have assumed that there was more than friendship between them and would have crossed her off any list he might be keeping of eligible women.

Not that he kept such a list.

Actually, he did have a list. Eleanor was the only one on it.

"Thank you for meeting me. I had so many things I wanted to talk to you about, and a phone call just doesn't work whenever you have things that you have to show people and say to them." Maisie picked up the bag that she dropped in her excitement to meet him apparently.

"And I want you to see my dress. I was hoping that you would have a tie in your closet that would match it. I think that would look striking, don't you? We talked about matching before, and we've just never been coordinated enough. But now that I have my dress, if you don't think you have a tie, we can pick one up quickly. It's a deep plum color, and I'm sure we'll find a tie pretty easily." She laughed. "It's a popular color this year."

He wanted green. He liked green. Deep velvet green.

Maisie chattered on, and he tried to pay attention. They ordered their drinks, waited for them to be served, and found a table by the window.

When he looked out, of course, Eleanor was gone.

Maisie pulled her dress out of the bag and held it up. "Don't you just love this color?" she said with a big smile.

He tried to shake himself out of the funk he was in. Most of it having to do with the fact that he was pretty sure he had made the exact wrong decision. Yes, he and Maisie had been friends a lot longer than he and Eleanor, but with the clarity that comes from hindsight, he could see that Maisie had said she couldn't go. He had found someone else to go with. Someone who had said yes. He was going with her and had made that commitment. Obviously, he could see quite clearly now that he should have stuck with his commitment to Eleanor. For him to ditch her or to have broken off their deal, since he didn't feel like he exactly ditched her, in order to keep Maisie happy had been a mistake.

But there wasn't much he could do about it now. He'd made a bad decision, and he would have to live with it. He just... He wished there was something he could do to make it up to Eleanor.

But if he had to guess, she was probably feeling like she'd been shoved aside. Like someone else was more important than she was, and that's exactly how he'd acted. So it was only natural for her to feel that way.

"You're awfully quiet today. Is there something wrong?"

"Just a lot of my mind," he said.

"Of course. You currently have so many last-minute things you're doing with the gala. What about last year, when they called you at the last minute because no one had remembered to order any lights? And twinkle lights were the centerpiece of all the decorations? What a mess." Maisie shook her head, rolled her eyes, and laughed.

He had so much history with Maisie. They'd done so much together, and she was a nice woman. But... She just wasn't for him.

"Actually, I'm not feeling the greatest. Tomorrow's going to be a big day. Do you mind if I...leave?"

He was taking the easy way out. He didn't feel like talking, didn't want to force himself to be charming and kind when what he really wanted was to castigate himself for doing something stupid. And he was leaving in order to not have to keep up the pretense.

But Maisie's face registered concern immediately. "Of course. Tomorrow's a big day. The biggest of the year. We want everything to go without a hitch. I hope you're not getting sick."

"I hope I'm not either."

She picked up her drink and her bag, and they stood together.

He thought he caught a glimpse of a red coat, but there were several as they were exiting the shop. Surely Eleanor hadn't come into the coffee shop and he missed her? Of course, he'd been sitting with his back to the door. And as soon as he sat down, he'd looked for her and didn't see her. She could very well be in there.

Suddenly he was interested in staying, but they stepped out.

"Thanks a lot for all your help," he said, wanting to get away.

"I'll walk you to your office."

"I think I'm going to head to my condo. I'm going to lie down for a bit."

"You really aren't feeling well." The concern was back in her eyes as she laid a hand on his arm.

He wanted to shake it off. Maisie had never felt clingy before, but she did now. It was his fault. He should have been more clear. She wasn't doing anything wrong. Maybe a little more touchy-feely than what she usually was, but she had just been afraid that her sister was going to die. He couldn't blame her.

He assured her that he was fine, and she finally allowed him to walk away alone.

His phone buzzed in his pocket, and he thought about not answering it. He really did just want to be left alone.

But he pulled it out. It might be something about the gala that no one else could answer. He didn't want to keep things from progressing as smoothly as they could or make things harder for Lynette.

But it was his brother, Peter.

He laughed. He hadn't even talked to Peter before he left Strawberry Sands. His whole thought and being had been focused on Eleanor.

"Hello?"

"Hey, bro. Heard you had a cold night."

"Actually, it wasn't cold at all." He thought about the fire and holding Eleanor on the floor underneath the blankets. It had actually been a pretty good night. Maybe a little bit uncomfortable, because the floor was hard and they didn't have pillows, but...a night of good memories.

"Must've been some fire. That's a small stove. Anyway, just wanted to check and make sure you were okay."

"Well, I'm not dead, so I guess I must be okay."

Peter was often the first to crack a joke, but no one on earth knew him better than his brother. Even though they'd chosen very different paths, with Peter deciding to become a farmer, taking classes in vocational agriculture and earning a degree in animal science, and Franklin going the business route, they were still as close as brothers could be.

Now Peter was serious.

"All right. I know you have a gala tomorrow, and you're probably thinking about that, but there's something else going on."

He laughed to himself. He really didn't need to talk to anyone who knew him so well.

But Peter always saw things with a clarity that Franklin sometimes missed. He couldn't think of anyone else that he would trust with the information that he suddenly realized he was going to divulge to his brother.

"I always go to the gala with Maisie. But she called me and couldn't go because her sister was sick."

"The one that's in Africa?"

"Yeah, that one. She was going to catch the first plane she could and go see her. So I was dateless."

"Ouch. It's always harder to do those things solo. Even if your date isn't someone that you're in a relationship with, it's just nice to have that support beside you."

"Exactly. So, since I was with Eleanor last night—"

"Eleanor. She's a nice girl."

"She was. She planned the barn dance and did a fabulous job on it."

"I thought so. I had a great time. Of course, I wasn't abducted by accident either, so there's that."

Franklin snorted. "I actually really didn't mind."

"That's shocking to me. But I want to know what you said to Eleanor."

"I asked her if she'd go. If she'd be my date."

"Wow. You guys must have had some pretty deep conversations last night."

"It was an easy thing to do. I didn't have a phone, and she was the only one available." It went deeper than that, but he didn't want to admit it.

"What did she say? Did she turn you down? Is that what the problem is? Turned down by a small-town girl?"

"No. She said yes. That's not the problem."

"Now you can't figure out how to get her there? Do you need me to drive her down tomorrow?"

"No. The problem is Maisie's sister wasn't as sick as what she thought, and Maisie called me and said she could go."

"Well, too bad. You already asked Eleanor, and she said yes. So Maisie is out of luck."

"Why couldn't you have told me that two hours ago?"

"Are you serious?"

"Yeah. I mean, Maisie is the one I always go with. I mean, she's good at it, she's always done well, and we have an understanding. I didn't want to miss any of that. She could benefit me in my career. Not to mention, if I hurt her feelings, she could go around and make things really difficult for me."

"I don't think you need to worry about any of that. Whether she does or she doesn't, it doesn't matter. She told you she couldn't go, and you asked Eleanor. She said yes. You can't break off with Eleanor just because something better came along. Or just because Maisie can do it again. You have to keep your word. If you said you were going to do it, you need to do it."

"But I asked Eleanor, told her about Maisie, and asked her if it was okay if I went with Maisie. She said it was fine. I just…feel like I made the wrong choice, even though I was going with Maisie and being loyal to her."

"But you weren't being loyal to Eleanor, whom you gave your word to. You might not have known her for as long, but there is a loyalty in doing what you say you're going to do, even when it's hard. Or even when something else better comes along and you want to do that."

Franklin was quiet. He knew that Peter was correct.

"I mean, I know you think you asked her and she said it was okay and all that, but what else was she supposed to say? Did you actually think she was going to say 'no, don't go with Maisie? You promised me?' And why would she want to have to force you to keep your promise to her?" He snorted. "She probably figured if you don't want her, you don't want her."

"But I asked her out. I told her I wanted her!"

"Your actions—the fact that you had someone else lined up and were going to replace her if she just said the word—said you didn't."

He didn't mean to argue. He just…wished it wasn't so obvious now. What had been obscure to him before. He had been surprised, he supposed, and that's maybe why he didn't make the best decision that he could have.

He didn't know what else to blame it on. Maybe he wasn't supposed to blame it on anything. Maybe he was supposed to take the blame for it, admit it, and then…what?

"I screwed up."

"I think that's the first step in fixing things," Peter said easily.

"What's the next step?" Franklin said, laughing a little. That was his problem. He didn't know what to do to fix it.

"I don't know. I guess apologizing."

"Yeah. Okay, that makes sense." Definitely he needed to apologize. He was an idiot. But maybe it hadn't hurt her feelings as much as he thought. If she had done to him what he just did to her, it definitely would have upset him and hurt his feelings. Even if they'd only been friends, and here he was hoping for more. Not that he would have admitted it to anyone.

"Then what?"

"Man, I don't know," Peter said, sounding exasperated and amused at the same time. "I'm not married. Maybe that's why. I guess... I guess you just need to try to show her that you're going to try to do better. I mean, you can say it, but until she actually sees you trying to do something better? It doesn't really mean anything, you know? Anybody can apologize. Although some people don't. And anybody can say they're going to try to do better. Just like anybody can say thank you. It's just a matter of...showing your thanks."

Great, now he had to try to figure out how to show that he was actually remorseful. But how did he do that? It wasn't like he could drum up another situation where he had to choose between Eleanor and someone else and he would choose Eleanor.

Man, he had a golden opportunity to show her how much he thought of her, and he'd screwed it up.

Still, he figured Peter was right. He just needed to watch for the opportunity and, in the meantime, do his best to show her that he was remorseful and that she truly did mean something to him.

It bothered him that she wasn't going to be at his gala and hadn't wanted to go out with him again. But he could try to run into her in other situations, until maybe she changed her mind.

He hoped that would work, since he couldn't think of anything else, and he hadn't realized until that point how much he liked Eleanor.

Chapter 17

"Do you think I'm wrong?" Eleanor asked Sunday as they got in the elevator to go up to their hotel rooms.

Noah had a meeting, although he was going to be along later. For the moment, it was just the two of them, and Eleanor had all of Sunday's attention.

But Sunday had been quiet, thoughtful, and that had made Eleanor start thinking about how she'd handled things.

Maybe she'd done it wrong.

"What makes you ask that?" Sunday said, without giving anything away.

She waited for Eleanor to get on the elevator before she punched the number to their floor.

"I don't know. I guess I've just been thinking that I wasn't a very good friend. I mean, I know I haven't known him for very long, but last night, I kept thinking that I felt like we formed a bond. Not necessarily a romantic bond," she hurried to add when Sunday raised her brows. "Just... Just we'd done something hard together, and I enjoyed his company, and he said he enjoyed mine, and I thought we were friends."

"You probably are," Sunday said simply.

"But I'm not acting like a friend, am I?"

Sunday didn't say anything. She just smiled.

"Yeah. You agree. I was petulant. He didn't treat me the way I thought I should be treated, and so instead of supporting him like a friend would, I...walked away."

"I think some of us have a personality where we avoid conflict or difficult situations by walking away from them. Some people live for confrontations. You just did what was natural to you. But I'm glad you're thinking about it, because I'm not sure it was right."

"If we're friends, it definitely wasn't right." Eleanor had to admit she was mumbling. She wasn't proud of what she had done. She'd allowed her hurt feelings to dictate her actions, instead of overlooking herself and focusing on someone else. The gala meant a lot to Franklin. It was the big thing for his company every year. He was doing his best for it, and if she was his friend, she'd be supporting him, not pouting in some corner because he didn't treat her right.

The elevator stopped, and an older couple waited while Sunday and Eleanor got out.

They were a sweet couple, gray and stooped, but still holding hands. The older gentleman said something, and the lady beside him laughed. They got on the elevator, and as Sunday and Eleanor walked away, their laughter followed them down the hall.

That's what she wanted for herself. A love that lasted through the decades, from their young adult years, through middle age, and into their golden years. She wanted someone beside her. Someone holding her hand. Someone to laugh with.

The longing was so strong, she almost stopped in the middle of the hall.

She wanted someone to love her the way she was, but she also wanted to be the kind of woman who deserved a man who would stand beside her, laugh with her, and love her despite her faults and flaws.

She could hardly expect that kind of treatment out of her future husband, whoever he was, if that wasn't the kind of friend that she was today.

Being a friend was a lot different than being a husband or wife, but it took the same kind of character. The kind of character that put others ahead of themselves, the kind of character that God wanted her to have.

They reached her room, and she paused for a moment, grabbing her card from her wallet while Sunday looked for hers.

"Will you hate me if I change my mind again?" Eleanor asked as she shuffled her bags around and got her card in her hand.

"You know I won't. Sometimes we just do the wrong thing, make the wrong decision, and we have to check ourselves and turn around. Why would that make me mad?"

"Because I feel like I've jerked you one way and then another. Here you are in Chicago, not because you want to be, but because of me."

"Noah was going to go to the gala tomorrow anyway."

"I know, but you could be with your husband, or taking a nap, or doing something."

"There aren't too many things I'd rather do than be with my sister," Sunday said as she put her arm around Eleanor's shoulders.

Eleanor leaned into her, saying a silent prayer of thanks to God for giving her sisters. They were better than friends.

"I want to go to the gala," she said as Sunday's hand dropped and she pulled away.

"I thought that's what you were going to say."

"Thanks. I just... I just feel like that's the thing that a friend would do. And that's what I want to be. A good friend." For some reason, her heart still hurt, and she wasn't sure if it was just her woman's pride being tweaked because Franklin had basically dumped her over someone else, or whether it was because she actually had feelings for Franklin. Which she felt wasn't very smart since she'd only spent a little bit of time with him.

But it was time in trying circumstances. A person's worst side came out when they were squeezed the way they had been squeezed last night. Cold, hungry, put out, scared, and challenged. She could see what kind of stuff he was made of, and she really liked it.

"I can't believe you didn't get upset about everything last night. That's probably the thing that impressed me the most."

"Franklin is so easygoing. He was really able to roll with things."

"That's something that Noah has said about him over and over. And it's something that I've seen in the few times I've interacted with him. He doesn't get angry. In fact, I'm not sure Noah has ever seen him angry."

"I guess anger is an emotion that humans are allowed to feel. I don't hold that against anyone. I get angry. But it was just really nice to spend the night with someone who wasn't holding it against anyone, who didn't sit around and complain, who let it all slide, and just focused on what we needed to do. On being a decent human being, rather than on all the things he deserved but didn't get."

"In other words, he was humble and resourceful and the kind of companion you want to spend more time with."

"Yeah."

Maybe Sunday suspected that she might have been falling a little bit in love with Franklin. Who wouldn't be after what she experienced with him?

She supposed that was only natural.

"Noah said he'd like to leave by six tomorrow. Does that work for you?"

"Of course," Eleanor said, smiling with relief.

"I'll plan to be over at five thirty to do your hair. After all, if you're going to support Franklin, you want to look your best."

There was a little bit of humor twinkling in Sunday's eyes, and Eleanor figured she suspected there was more to it than just being friends.

But that's all Eleanor wanted to be. She didn't want to be hopelessly in love with someone who could never return those feelings. Of course, sometimes a person couldn't control how they felt. But she could control what she did. God was clear about that.

She said goodbye to her sister, pushed her door open, and closed it behind her.

She could control her actions, and so she would.

The next day, she, Sunday, and Noah enjoyed a late brunch and then spent some time sightseeing before returning to the hotel to get ready. It didn't take Eleanor too long to change into her dress, and she paced back and forth in her room until her sister arrived. If Sunday noticed her agitation at all, she didn't comment on it, just smiled and chatted as she gave Eleanor's hair a proper makeover.

Later that night, Noah pulled up to the gala, with Sunday in the front seat beside him. Eleanor sat in the back, her heart beating hard.

She wasn't sure why she was nervous. No one would be looking at her. No one would care.

It was probably just the idea of seeing Franklin again. Which was a little scary. She didn't want to be so invested in him.

But she did want to support him. This was a big deal for him, and maybe seeing a friendly face would make his evening a little brighter.

Maybe they could share a smile over the night they'd shared recently.

Regardless, she pushed her nerves aside and got out, standing beside Sunday as Noah handed the keys to the valet.

He came up beside them, and Sunday put her hand in the crook of his arm. She put her other arm around Eleanor, and the three of them walked up the sidewalk to the front doors.

Eleanor was thankful for her new dress. It gave her confidence. Made her feel like even if she wasn't exactly on the same plane as these people, she didn't feel like she was at such a disadvantage.

It was obviously a place where everyone was expecting to have fun. There were smiles and laughter, and people looked eager for the evening to start.

"Noah said that this is the highlight of the Christmas season for Chicago," Sunday said as she leaned her head down and spoke in Eleanor's ear.

"I believe it. It just feels so...festive." In a big-city kind of way. It wasn't the cozy, small-town atmosphere, but it felt Christmasy all the same. Bright lights, decorated trees, gifts artistically arranged around them, the smell of good food and the sound of laughter and the dulcet tones of Christmas music waved through the air.

She wasn't sure she'd ever been anywhere more magical.

They walked in, and it was hard for Eleanor to absorb it all. They were offered food from trays and drinks from the same, there were people on the dance floor dancing, and others sitting in seats, either watching the dancers or with food in front of them while they laughed and chatted with their neighbors.

Eleanor had a hard time resisting a table where the most delicious-looing pieces of key lime pie sat, artfully arranged. She promised herself she'd grab a slice before the evening was out.

Noah casually led them to the room where the silent auction was going on. Tables lined the entire periphery of the room, with gifts and other goodies piled high. In front of each lot was a code they could scan with their phone that would take them to a website where they could punch in their offer.

Eleanor put her hands behind her back as she perused some of the offerings.

Her eye caught on a figure dressed in black, tall and confident, and she peered through the crowd to try to see him again.

She was pretty sure it was Franklin. She wanted to wish him well. Wanted to tell him that she hoped his evening was amazing and his whole gala was a success. Wanted him to know that she supported him, no matter what.

"He's over there. I just texted him, and he's making his way this way," Noah said as he and Sunday, who had browsed in the opposite direction, met Eleanor on the other side of the room.

Somehow his words made a big lump of nervousness explode in her stomach. It dripped down, coating her entire insides, until she wanted to put both hands over her stomach to try to ease the uncomfortable sensation.

That was silly. The man she was going to talk to was the same man who helped her deliver a kitten, made a fire, and snuggled under the blankets to keep warm and not freeze to death. He was the exact same man.

He was also the man who had asked her to go with him and then changed his mind and made an awkward phone call to her where he basically asked her to back out so he could take someone else when the someone else he preferred above her was able to do it instead.

She tried not to think of that. It wasn't a date. It was just him doing his auction and trying to make it as successful as possible. And she was just being the best friend she could.

Why was she trying to be such a good friend to someone who hadn't been a good friend to her? She knew that was a question the rest of the world would ask. After all, wasn't the point of friendship to have someone who had your back and whom you could trust? Obviously, Franklin didn't have her back since he'd all but ditched her as soon as someone who would serve him better came along.

But...wasn't that what being a Christian was all about? She wasn't supposed to worry about the way she was treated. Instead, she was to love with the kind of love Jesus showed to his disciples. Jesus's disciples hadn't treated Jesus well at all—they'd deserted him in his time of greatest need, but he'd loved them anyway.

And that's the kind of love Jesus modeled because that's the kind of love he wanted his followers to show. To give the kind of love that didn't ask for anything in return.

She kept her hands behind her back and strolled on down the table, looking at all of the amazing things being offered at the silent auction. There was a cruise to the Bahamas and another one to Alaska. There were dresses and boots, packages of perfumes which she assumed were expensive, and even a week at a condo in Italy.

High-end type gifts that she would never even dream of. If she had donated something to the auction, it would have been something small, like a free dog grooming for one pet or something like that.

But these, these were huge.

It made her feel like even though she had wanted to think of herself as one of Franklin's friends, she really wasn't on the same playing field as he was at all. The stuff was so...extra. So much beyond what she thought of in her little world.

Chapter 18

"**H**ey there."

Eleanor recognized Franklin's voice right away, and it sent some kind of friction of something that felt a lot like alarm wrapped in velvet down her backbone.

She took a breath and turned. Franklin stood there, looking so much different than he had the last time she'd seen him. He wore a tux, very formal, with a bow tie, and he filled it out very nicely. His white shirt contrasted with the tan of his skin and the rugged stubble that lined his cheeks and chin.

His lips turned up in a ghost of a smile, but his eyes seemed worried. "I wasn't expecting to see you."

"This is an important day for you. I told you I was a friend, but I wouldn't have been acting like a friend if I hadn't been here to support you, would I?" She wanted her words to be cheerful and happy and upbeat and like she didn't have a care in the world, and like it hadn't been an agonizing decision to come here when her heart hurt so much.

She didn't quite succeed. Her words weren't sad, but they were soft and thoughtful rather than upbeat and happy.

"That's very big of you. But after what I saw the other night, it's exactly something I would expect from you."

His words made her happy, but they also made her feel guilty. He didn't understand the struggle that she had with herself to get to this spot. He made it sound like this was her choice all along.

She shook her head. "I don't deserve that."

"You do. Especially..." He put his hands behind his back and took a breath, like he was trying to find the right words or maybe get up the nerve to say whatever it was he was going to say. "I was able to see clearly that I handled everything all wrong. I... I thought I was being loyal to someone who has been loyal to me, but in doing that, I... I didn't treat you the way you should have been treated. I wish I could go back and do it differently. It's obvious to me now that once you said yes, I should have stuck with you. I should never have put that pressure on you. I shouldn't have even asked you if it was okay. It's obvious to me now that doing that left you no choice but to say yes. And that was nice for me, because then I didn't have to say no to Maisie. I'm sorry."

She blinked. Trying to comprehend what he was saying. He had apologized? He had said he was wrong? "No. You wanted to do this with Maisie, and she knew exactly how to do everything you needed. It's the way it needed to be."

"No. You misunderstand. I wanted to go with you. I didn't want to hurt Maisie, and I knew she could jump in and do the gala easily, but I took the coward's way out by asking you if it was okay. You couldn't have said anything except yes without feeling like you were not being kind to me. It was wrong of me to expect you to do that."

She swallowed. His words had clogged up her throat. Still, a part of her wanted to be standoffish. Didn't want to put it behind her so easily, to give him a free pass to...hurt her again? She didn't think he was that kind of man, but other people had done the same thing to her.

It felt like when a person forgave too easily, they were giving the person a pass to do the exact same thing over again because there were no consequences. She wanted to be the one to inflict the consequences, but just as soon as she thought that, she remembered. *Vengeance is mine; I will repay, saith the Lord.*

Right away, she prayed a quick, silent prayer, *God, no, please, I don't want any vengeance for him. Please don't. I forgive. Please forget.*

"I forgive you. Although, I don't know that there was anything to forgive." Sure, he'd hurt her feelings, but that was her, not him.

She wanted to talk more, wanted to work things out in her mind. After all, she was still his second choice. He had his mouth open to say something else when Noah and Sunday came over, holding hands.

"You've outdone yourself this year," Noah said, clapping his hand down on Franklin's shoulder.

Franklin's eyes held hers for just another short moment before he smiled and turned to his friend. "I just have the right PR company. They did an awesome job."

"You can say that if you want to, but I know there's work behind the scenes that you do. Sure, they put these things together, but someone has to spearhead everything, organize it, and fund it. I know it's not cheap."

Franklin didn't say much to that, just nodded. Which made Eleanor wonder exactly how much something like this cost. She hadn't considered the money that it took to put this on. But not only was he earning money for a good cause, but people were having a fantastic time. If the happy looks on people's faces were any indication. She supposed some people really did enjoy this type of thing, and Franklin not only set aside the time and the effort to make it happen, but he bankrolled it as well. Maybe other people, like her, never stopped to consider the financial contributions he made.

Noah and Franklin talked for just a bit more before someone caught Noah's attention, and they moved away with them.

"I really appreciate you coming tonight," Franklin said once Noah and Sunday had moved away.

"I'm glad I did. It's definitely fun to see you not in a shack, not tending a fire, not delivering kittens. But in your element. You look comfortable and like you belong here." Those words were sincere.

His hand reached up and touched the skin of her arm just below where the sleeve of her jacket stopped. "I... I really would like to spend more time with you. I know that you already turned me down, and I don't want to be annoying, but...maybe sometime?"

She smiled. She appreciated the fact that he hadn't been put off by being turned down once. That he saw her being here as what it was, her realizing that she'd been wrong. And that he wanted to be with her so much that he was willing to try again, risk rejection again.

Was she?

Maybe it was her heart that spoke. "I'd like that."

He opened his mouth, but someone else called his name, and while Franklin didn't look to begin with, they called it again, more insistently.

"I have to go." He didn't look like he wanted to.

She nodded. "This is your night. Enjoy. And congratulations, from where I stand, it's a resounding success."

"Somehow, where you stand is really important to me."

With those words, that she wasn't quite sure what they meant, he turned and walked away.

She spent most of the rest of the night smiling. It helped that she moved about, finding a seat at a table in the corner where she could look out over most of the room and caught lots of glimpses of Franklin. Him laughing and mingling, him working with what she assumed was the event coordinator behind the scenes as he directed different things. She couldn't hear what he was saying, but she could see his hands move, see him point, see him smile and nod.

Funny how much she enjoyed just watching.

Then, an hour after the silent auction closed, a woman that Eleanor assumed was Maisie called for everyone's attention from the low stage at the front of the room.

By that time, Noah and Sunday had joined her at the table, and they each had a glass of punch in front of them as well as some hors d'oeuvres from the side table.

"Can I have your attention please?" Maisie said, sounding confident and totally at ease standing in front of such a huge crowd of people and talking.

Of course she sounded confident; she'd done this before with Franklin, and that was part of the reason he continued to have her. She did a good job. She was good at what she did.

Eleanor hoped it wasn't jealousy that ran through her.

She was good at what she did too. Grooming animals, mostly dogs. This certainly wasn't anything that she was good at. She'd felt uncomfortable most of the evening and had had to push that feeling aside. She did enjoy herself, sure, but she had been thankful more than once that she hadn't actually had to do anything. She wouldn't have had the first idea of how to handle all the things that Maisie had been doing all evening.

Maisie had been as busy as Franklin, and Eleanor would be remiss if she didn't give Maisie credit for being busy the entire evening.

"Congratulations, Franklin, on another successful charity event. Let's give him a round of applause."

The entire room erupted in clapping. Including Eleanor and Sunday and Noah. Noah especially looked proud of his friend and business partner.

"I have the results of the silent auction, and everyone who won will be sent a text message shortly. Everything is automated this year, which made things a lot quicker and easier." There was laughter that rippled through the crowd.

"I'll put the winners up on the screen so everyone can see, and I'll put the winning bids up as well. So you can see how far you fell short." More laughter.

"And now, since we have some extra time, I have a little personal thing I want to do." She took a breath, and for the first time, Eleanor wondered if maybe she was nervous and just really good at hiding it. "For years, Franklin and I have been doing this together. Actually, Franklin and I have been doing a lot of things together. We've gone to different business functions together, holiday parties, and this is the crowning moment every year. It's been a joy to have him by my side, and..." She smiled and turned to Franklin, the hand that wasn't holding her microphone reaching out and clasping his.

Franklin's expression could only be described as shocked as her fingers touched his and their hands clasped. Up until that point, he'd been smiling and laughing with everyone else, enjoying Maisie doing what she was obviously very good at.

"I've been thinking for a while that I want us to be more. How about it, Franklin? Do you want to make our successful business collaboration a more personal and successful collaboration? I'd like to be exclusive."

Somehow her voice dropped on that last sentence, and she made it sound almost sexy.

Eleanor's eyes blinked. Her heart fluttered. She hadn't been expecting this. Not at all. And after the way Franklin had talked to her, asking her out again, making her feel like he actually wanted to be with her, she'd allowed herself to think that maybe the little bit that she was falling for him was okay.

Lord, I thought You threw us together for a reason. I thought I was walking in the exact spot You wanted me to be. I thought... I thought my feelings were actually right for once.

She wanted Franklin to renounce everything that Maisie had said or at least to let her down. She didn't want Maisie to be embarrassed. She didn't want Franklin to do the verbal equivalent of a body slam on the carpet. But she did want Franklin to be very clear that he wasn't interested in Maisie. Not like that. Only in a business sense.

But Franklin didn't say anything.

The crowd erupted in cheers as the smile on Maisie's face grew large, and she tugged on his hand.

Maybe she caught him off balance, that's what Eleanor wanted to think, because he took a step forward, although it wasn't very graceful.

She finished closing the distance between them, threw her arms around his neck, and...

Eleanor looked away. It was like a car accident, only she couldn't watch. She didn't want to see how it ended. She didn't want that image to be seared into her mind; she didn't want to feel worse than what she already did.

Would it be terrible for her to leave now?

She wanted to go. She just wanted to go and hide in her hotel room, crawl under the covers, cry into her pillow. This felt worse than it had felt earlier, because she thought Franklin had given her hope.

The orchestra struck up a romantic song, and the dance floor was flooded with bodies. People stood from their tables, and Eleanor no longer had to worry about averting her eyes because she couldn't see anything.

"Do you think we could go? I... I'm so tired," Sunday said, and Eleanor wanted to reach over the table and hug her.

Sunday wasn't tired. Sunday was fine. But Sunday knew Eleanor wasn't.

"Of course. I texted the valet, and he'll have our car by the time we get to the door. We can go now."

Noah stood up from the table, so they did as well, and Eleanor willed her legs to work. She just needed them to work until they got to the hotel and she got upstairs to her room. Once she closed the door behind her, then her legs could do whatever they wanted to, which was fold up into a heap on the floor.

It was a short walk to the entryway, but as they stepped in, Sunday said, "I'm so sorry, but do you mind if I use the restroom before we go?"

Normally Eleanor would have gone with her, but she barely heard and allowed Sunday to walk away while she stood dazed. She wanted things to be different. Wanted to believe Franklin when he'd said that he really preferred her even though he'd chosen to go with Maisie.

"Eleanor?" Noah's voice penetrated her thoughts. She looked up.

"Yes?"

"I hesitated to say anything, because if there is anyone worse at relationships and love than me, I've never found them."

She tried to smile, since that seemed like a bit of humor. Unfortunately it seemed to come out more like a grimace.

"But Franklin is my friend and business partner for a reason - he's a good man. He has integrity and character and he always tries to do the right thing. Just...sometimes he makes wrong choices."

She stared at her brother-in-law. Was he saying she should forgive this, too?

"I'm not disagreeing, but I think he's made his preference very clear."

"Are you talking about me?"

Her head jerked around. Franklin had come out to the deserted entryway, breathing hard, like he'd run for blocks to catch her. Or maybe he'd just done something really hard. Like walk away from Maisie in front of all those people.

"I'm going to meet Sunday. We'll be outside. Take your time. Good luck, bro." She barely noticed when Noah walked away after clapping a hand down on Franklin's shoulder.

Eleanor stared at him, and he looked steadily back at her, their eyes meeting and holding while her heart pounded furiously in her chest and her palms started to sweat.

"You're not dancing with Maisie."

"No."

Her throat was too tight to swallow.

He tugged at the collar of his shirt.

"I hated to embarrass her in front of everyone, but I'd already made one mistake with her that hurt you. I wasn't making another. Didn't you hear my response?"

"No." She had been in such a rush to get out, just trying to keep her legs holding her weight without collapsing.

One side of his mouth flattened. "I told her no. That there was someone else. Someone I should have been with to begin with."

She closed her eyes. She didn't want Maisie to be embarrassed, but this was what she needed - Franklin to put her first.

"Are you okay?" He moved closer, putting a tentative hand on her arm.

Her eyes pricked as she opened them, filling up because of the happiness in her chest that couldn't be contained.

"You chose me?"

Was it terrible that so much of how she felt hinged on his decision? Shouldn't she be happy no matter what?

But it was natural for her to want the man she loved...her eyes widened. Did she love Franklin?

"Yes. I chose you. Just like I should have two days ago. I couldn't fix that mistake, but I can try hard not to make it again." His thumb brushed along her arm, sending a soft thrill up her arm and through her chest. "I want to be with you. Tonight. Tomorrow. The next day...And anytime we're snowed in, too."

She brushed at the corner of her eye and gave a watery chuckle.

"Is that just because you know I don't hog the blankets so you know you're not in any danger of freezing to death?"

"That might be part of the reason." He stepped closer. Her breath caught and her smile faded. "But only because that shows me what kind of character you really have. The kind where you put others first, even if it means you'll end up cold. How can I get snowed in with someone like that and not fall in love with them?"

Her mouth opened and her body froze.

He moved closer. His hand slid from her arm to her waist.

"I know you might not feel the same, especially after what I did earlier this week. I was stupid and wrong and you can't believe how sorry I am about that. I'm just hoping and praying that you'll give me another chance. I want to show you that you're more important to me than anything or anyone else. I know I can tell you, but I showed you something different this week. I can't expect you to forget so soon and I don't blame you for not believing me. I'm willing to wait as long as it takes for you to see, and maybe feel something for me, even half of what I feel for you. I love you."

She blinked, trying to take it all in. He had apologized. Had asked her to forgive him. Wanted to wait for her to feel the same...

"I do feel the same!" She put a hand on his chest. "I thought God was clearly telling me that you were perfect for me, but when you chose Maisie...I thought I was wrong."

"You weren't!" His eyes pleaded. "I just made a stupid decision. The wrong decision. It was...easier. And easier is usually not better."

"I'd already forgiven you. But I thought, after tonight and what Maisie just said, that you truly wanted her and I was wrong."

"You weren't!"

She smiled. He was out here with her, rather than dancing with Maisie. "I know."

"Does that mean I still have a chance with you?"

"How could I turn down someone whom I know doesn't hog the covers? Who delivers kittens and gets up in the middle of the night to fix the fire and snuggles with me to keep me warm?"

"It wasn't a hardship." His lips smiled, even as his head lowered.

"Good to know," she murmured just before his lips touched hers and his arms pulled her tight and she buried her hands in his hair and forgot about the gala and Maisie and her sister and husband who were waiting on her, and just pressed herself to Franklin, not able to get close enough, hold tight enough, or get enough air to breathe.

She pulled back, trembling a little. "I love you."

"I know. The kind of love that has you here to support me, even after I hurt you and acted like an idiot. Don't you know how beautiful and amazing that is to me?"

She bit her lip, willing her eyes not to fill with tears again. He didn't know how close she was to not coming.

He continued, not needing her to say anything. "I don't want to take advantage of someone who will stick beside me like that, but I also don't want to lose you. Whatever it takes to keep you, to be with you, to learn to love you in the exact same way, I'm willing to do anything, because having someone like you beside me is priceless. I don't deserve it."

Maybe they were the words she needed to hear, but more than words, she needed to have him choose her, not because it was convenient or easy, but because he wanted to. That, more than all the words in the world, made her heart sing and her spirit know for sure that Franklin was the one who brought light to her life.

"Tonight was enough." That was all she could say. But he understood, because he smiled, and his eyes crinkled, while his arms tightened around her.

"Thank you."

They looked into each other's eyes, the faint strains of the music drifting through the closed doors as they said so much to each other without saying anything at all. Commitment and sacrifice and the light of love weaving through the air between them. Eleanor had never felt anything like it, but more than that feeling, was the sure knowledge that Franklin was a good man, a man of character and integrity, who loved God and would stay beside her and choose her over everything and everyone else. What more could she ask for?

Epilogue

Pam Corrigan stood beside her best friend, Mark Shields as they softly sang Silent Night with the rest of the congregation who had gathered at the church in Strawberry Sands on Christmas Eve.

She'd lived for over a half a century and Christmas Eve had always been her favorite day of the year. It was always extra sweet to spend it with Mark, her best friend for the last decade. Although she wished her girls had come home. But they were with her mother and would be coming tomorrow for dinner.

And she would survive another Christmas after her cheating husband had divorced her.

She hadn't expected to spend her life alone. Not after she'd gotten married and pledged her life to someone.

But she had Mark. He'd be there, too. Which was great. Maybe she'd be able to talk to him about the conditions at the school where she taught. The older administrators had been retiring one by one, with new, younger ones taking over. This year had been the worst yet. She wasn't allowed to talk to the children about the Lord, and she'd been told she couldn't have her Bible at her desk, nor offer any advice that hinted of religion.

She'd been quoted the fake wall of separation that did not appear in any founding documents.

Mark would ease her mind. He always did. He'd talk her out of quitting her job and using her savings to buy the old inn. She knew it was foolish to even think about doing that, but every time she did, it felt like exactly the right thing to do.

Her eyes moved from the sparkling candles in the corner to Eleanor and Franklin, who stood in the row ahead of her and to the left, holding hands and glowing like a couple in love.

Pam wouldn't mind getting stranded in a snowstorm with a great guy who would then fall in love with her and make her as happy as Eleanor obviously was.

Of course, that kind of thing didn't happen to normal people like her, although she was happy for Eleanor, who deserved every happiness.

At least she had a solid, life time friend in Mark. She looked over at him again. He wasn't exactly handsome, but he was loyal and fun and he made her laugh. Plus, he loved the Lord and knew the Bible as well as anyone she knew. He always gave her the best advice and listened to her problems, really listened.

She was blessed to have a neighbor like him. She advised herself to be happy with her blessings and not worry about the things she didn't have. A good friend was far better than a bad husband. She ought to know.

Enjoy this preview of *There I Find Patience,* just for you!

There I Find Patience

Chapter 1

She had just made a terrible mistake.

Pam Corrigan held the key that she'd been given at the closing in her hand.

What had she been thinking?

She sighed deeply and got out of her car, crossing the sidewalk and going up the steps to the duplex she shared with her best friend, Mark Shields.

Mark owned the duplex, and when Pam's marriage had blown up ten years ago, Mark had offered to allow her to move in to the other side which happened to be vacant at the time.

Pam had moved out of Strawberry Sands when she got married, and hadn't pictured herself moving back in. But with two teenage girls and nowhere else to turn, she'd taken Mark up on his offer, thinking it was only a temporary thing.

Temporary had turned into a decade.

"Good morning, Pam," Miss Heather called over. Miss Heather lived in the large house across the street with her granddaughter and her husband and several other older ladies. It wasn't exactly an assisted living facility, but it probably could have been.

Regardless, Miss Heather was a neighbor and a good one, and Pam turned, placing a smile on her face and waving across the street.

She hadn't seen Miss Heather nor Miss Daisy sitting on the porch, enjoying one of the rare warm April days.

April was just as likely to be below freezing as above eighty in Western Michigan along the lake.

So, when a person got a warm, beautiful day like today, they needed to get out and enjoy it.

Or get out and go buy an inn, apparently.

Pam swallowed again. What had she done?

"It's a beautiful day," Miss Heather spoke across the deserted street.

"It sure is. Maybe I'll be out later on my front porch, too."

"Better hurry up. I heard there's a cold front moving in, and we're going to get some rain ahead of it," Miss Daisy said, nodding sagely. "My bones agree with the weather forecast for once."

"Thanks for the heads-up. I... I need to go inside for a bit. But I definitely want to enjoy this. Who knows when it'll be nice out again." She threw up her hand and waved before she hurried up the rest of the steps and opened the door to her side of the duplex.

Some duplexes had a wall down the middle of the porch, but no such thing separated Mark's side from hers.

In the summer, occasionally his nieces had visited from Ann Arbor where Mark's sister lived. They played with Pam's girls, and they'd always use the whole porch.

Mark had been easygoing and a great neighbor, and Pam hoped she'd been the same.

They hadn't been best friends when she moved in, but through the years, no one had supported her more.

If her girls needed a daddy to go to the daddy-daughter dance, Mark stepped in.

And if his nieces needed someone to bake cookies or be a room chaperone for their senior trip, Pam had naturally volunteered.

But now...what Pam had just done could ruin everything.

She threw her purse on the kitchen table as she walked through her duplex and out the back door.

Their backyard was large and fenced in, the entire thing. Again, no fence separated between her side of the yard and his side.

They had never needed a fence.

Sitting down, she held on tight to the key that she had seemed to be unable to let go of.

Why had she quit her job again? A secure job. One with a guaranteed pension. That, along with her Social Security, would give her plenty of security even if her daughters never moved back home.

Her empty nest had been hard for the last two years since her youngest daughter graduated from college and moved out permanently.

Sure, the girls came home for holidays, most of them anyway, and sometimes for birthdays. Definitely for Pam's. But they had lives of their own, careers they cared about, and friends and hobbies that didn't include their mother anymore.

Pam really wasn't bothered by it most of the time. After all, she wouldn't want her children to be stuck at home, afraid to go out and do anything or go anywhere.

Although, she really wouldn't mind spending more time with them. And wouldn't have minded at all if they had chosen to stay at home and start their careers there.

She missed them.

Maybe that was why she had done what she did.

Was this what a midlife crisis looked like?

"Hey there."

The voice made her smile. Mark somehow always steadied her nerves. She'd been through the typical teenage drama and angst that every parent had gone through. Mark had spent more than one evening sitting at her table after the girls had gone to bed talking her down from a limb. Reminding her that everything passed, that a catastrophe today was something to laugh at tomorrow.

She appreciated his down-to-earth sensibility and the way he always made her problems seem like they weren't quite as bad as what she thought they were.

She wasn't sure how he was going to make her mother's reaction something that wasn't terrifying to her or convince her that she would eventually laugh at it, but if anyone could do it, Mark could.

"Hey," she said, trying not to sound depressed and petrified. The way she felt.

He finished walking out across his small back porch and sat down on the steps, on his side, with a good two feet between them.

They'd always been friends and nothing more. She appreciated his friendship more than she could say. Even now, knowing that she had just done something ridiculously dumb, just having him beside her made her feel... If not the smartest person in the world, at least like the repercussions of this day weren't the worst things that could happen to her.

"What's wrong?" he asked, not with alarm in his voice but with the confidence of someone who knew her.

Sometimes she loved having a friend who knew her so well that he knew something was wrong without words, and at other times, like now, it was a pain. What was she going to tell him?

"Just spit it out. I know you're sitting there wondering how you're going to tell me, and don't worry about it. Just tell me flat out."

She huffed out a breath and shook her head, looking over at him with a half-smile, half-exasperated look on her face. "Really? You have to read my mind today?"

"Pretty sure that's my job, isn't it?"

"No. Your job is to plant flowers and trees and make people's yards look beautiful. I'm pretty sure life counseling isn't in your job description."

His hands, work roughened and brown, rested on his leg while his boots were firmly planted on the step.

She always wondered why he didn't get married again. When she stopped to think about it, he was handsome. And kind, considerate, and sensitive. He was funny too and levelheaded. He had dated occasionally, different moms who were single and classmates of her daughters, but nothing ever stuck.

She wondered why.

Funny thing to wonder about now. Probably it was her brain trying to come up with a way to not answer his question.

"I do all those things, and I provide life counseling to a very elite group of people. Actually, that group includes just you."

"I can't complain about your life counseling. It's always been right on for me. But I feel bad that you even have to do it."

"I just like being involved in your life."

He was humble too. He was always able to give her good advice, because he was wise. He spent a lot of time with the Lord and in His Word, and that had a tendency to make a person wise.

"What did you do?"

"How do you know I did something?"

"Just a hunch," he said, humor in his voice.

"Well, it's a good one."

She'd done something terrible, and she was about to do something even worse.

She looked up, over the back of the fence, at the pasture that ran behind her house.

There were horses grazing in it, and the way the wind blew their manes and tails back soothed her soul almost as much as having Mark beside her.

He was quiet, knowing her well enough that he could probably read the signs that said she was trying to figure out where to start. Sometimes, it just took her a little bit to sort through the information in her brain and decide how to spit it all out.

"I quit my job."

"No." Disbelief forced the word out and wrapped his tones in shock.

"Yeah." She laughed a little, humorlessly, and lifted her gaze to meet his. "I told you it was bad."

"I knew there was a lot of stress there. But... I hadn't realized how much."

It was terrible to work somewhere where a person couldn't use their basic core beliefs to help any of the children. Things that she knew would help kids weren't allowed to be uttered in the classroom.

The previous principal at the school allowed them to talk about their faith and didn't get too concerned about it. But the new administration that had slowly been replacing the older folks as they retired had cracked down in a major way last year and this year. Being in the classroom was stressful enough, but she wasn't allowed to pray with the children, wasn't allowed to tell them that Jesus loved them, wasn't allowed to mention God at all. How did a person talk about science without mentioning God?

She always skipped over most of the parts of evolution in her science textbook. When she did mention it, she made sure to emphasize that it was a theory. In a small school like Blueberry Beach, where the school was located and where the kids from Strawberry Sands attended, folks would agree with stuff like that.

But her freedom to speak the Truth had been slowly taken away, and the stress had been getting to her. The workplace environment had gotten worse, even though there were many teachers who still got together in the mornings and had prayer for the students and Bible study together before the workday began.

Still, working in such an anti-Christian environment had taken its toll on her, along with the fact that her children were gone, and her life was…almost over. More than half over. It had been that way for a while, but the thoughts had been settling in all at once.

"I know. It's crazy, isn't it?" she said.

"I don't blame you. I don't think I could've worked as long as you did. When you're not allowed to talk about what you believe, and you're not allowed to share what you know will help the children who are having issues, it's really difficult."

She almost felt targeted and discriminated against. After all, pretty much anything else was perfectly okay to talk about.

Regardless, she tried to shove those thoughts aside.

"What did it drive you to do?" he asked again.

"I bought the inn."

"You didn't." His words were negative, but his tone held excitement. She could hear the pride in it. "I didn't think you would. But you did. That's awesome. Why are you so upset about it?"

"Because I quit my job."

"And you don't have enough money to live on and fix up the inn?"

"Yeah. What was I thinking? It's one thing to quit my job. It's another thing to buy the inn. But to do the two of them together? I am crazy."

Originally, when she talked about buying the inn, her thought had been to use her teacher salary to fix it up. After all, with both kids out of school and only one of her in the house, it didn't take nearly the money to run her household as it used to. Her grocery bill was down, light bill was also. The heating was cut in half, and she probably would never need to buy another item of clothing again.

But when she thought about buying the inn, she hadn't considered that she might quit her job too. That changed things.

JESSIE GUSSMAN

Pick up your copy of *There I Find Patience* by Jessie Gussman today!

A Gift from Jessie

View this code through your smart phone camera to be taken to a page where you can download a FREE ebook when you sign up to get updates from Jessie Gussman! Find out why people say, "Jessie's is the only newsletter I open and read" and "You make my day brighter. Love, love, love reading your newsletters. I don't know where you find time to write books. You are so busy living life. A true blessing." and "I know from now on that I can't be drinking my morning coffee while reading your newsletter – I laughed so hard I sprayed it out all over the table!"

Claim your free book from Jessie!